THE FRINGE SERIES

"Best science fiction I have read in a long while."
    ~Michael D. Griffiths, *SF Reader*

"*Fringe Runner* is epic fun with great characters, action, and suspense. Rachel Aukes is the next big name in the Space Opera genre!"
    ~ Nicholas Sansbury Smith, best-selling author of the *Extinction Cycle* series

"A perfect read for fans of the fantasy and sci-fi genres."
    ~ Ethan Gregory, *One Guy's Guide to Good Reads*

"I would recommend this novel to anyone who likes action-filled space operas and stories about fighting against the ruling government."
    ~ *Audiobook Reviewer*

EARTH UNDER SIEGE

"...Everything I've come to expect from this author. It's packed full of action, drama, surprise and suspense at every turn."
    ~*Silvia at Goodreads*

"Highly Recommended. Five Mysterious Stars."
    ~*RBS Productions*

"A top ten book!"
    ~ *Step into Fiction*

FRINGE STATION

FRINGE STATION

RACHEL AUKES

FRINGE STATION

Edited by Stephanie Riva, RivaReading.com and Laurel Kriegler, Kriegler Editing Services
Cover art © Vivid Covers | www.VividCovers.com

2nd edition 2022

ISBN: 978-0-9899018-7-1

For Brian, always.

CONTENTS

CHAPTER 1

SUPPLY RUN

THE *GRYPHON* SETTLED into position facing the *Honorless*, the most infamous pirate ship in the Collective.

Throttle powered down the navigational engines. "We're locked in and ready to play."

"Good work," Reyne said. He couldn't get a visual on Critch's ship—it was painted in a light-absorbing black and had no external lights on—but he knew the deadly craft stood fewer than fifty clicks off his bow.

He pulled up the sector grid on his panel. The *Honorless'* position was clearly marked by the largest blip. The *Gryphon* was a small blip directly across from it. Behind each of them, a line of seven ships branched outward—Critch's entire pirate fleet, known as the specters. Sixteen red blips in all formed a deadly funnel for anyone who made the mistake of entering it.

Reyne tapped each of the sixteen blips on his panel to manually mark each one's current position with a yellow halo.

The specters' private message channel lit up, and he read a broadcast from Critch:

Honorless: All ships are indicated in position. Hold position until tango passes you, then lock on to assigned coordinates. Tango will be on grid in five. Go silent NOW.

"It's time. Power down all external lights," Reyne ordered.

"Powering down now."

As she took care of the hull, he dimmed his instrument panel and the lights on the bridge. Throttle's pale white skin reflected the glow from her bright panel, while his dark skin and clothes blended into his black panel.

He turned off the ship's transponder and his craft's blip disappeared from the grid. One by one, the other fifteen red blips disappeared, leaving only the yellow circles he'd marked to indicate each ship's location.

He grabbed the comm and broadcast to the remaining two crew members on board. "Heads up. We're holding in position. The party starts in fifteen and should reach our doorstep in eighty minutes, so be ready. Sixx, wrap up whatever you're working on and make your way to the bridge. Comm silence for everyone from here on out."

Barely two minutes had passed before Throttle gave a drawn-out sigh. "I hate waiting."

Sixx stepped onto the bridge, chuckling. "That's because you were born without a milligram of patience. Remember that time you cut off a CUF patrol ship because you got tired of waiting for them to launch from Ice Port's docks?"

She rolled her eyes. "In my defense, he was flying like a ninety-year old grandpa. Plus, I was coming down with the flu and was feeling fidgety."

Sixx smiled as he strapped himself into his seat. "Fidgety? Sure, that must've been it."

"Run system checks, Throttle," Reyne said. "That should keep you busy for a couple more minutes at least."

"Already ran them."

"Run them again."

"Throttle's right," Sixx said. "Waiting sucks. We could all use some action."

"Be careful what you ask for." Reyne glanced over his shoulder. "Why don't you run weapons checks?"

"Already did, boss."

Reyne shot him a wry look.

Sixx held up his hands. "I know, I know. Run them again."

With his crew busy, Reyne found his attention drawn to the grid displayed on his panel, the only reminder that sixteen pirate ships waited, about to spring the biggest trap ever laid in the history of the fringe. Where most pirates were loners and outcasts, the specters were famed as the only organized pirate fleet. But they were pirates only to pass the time until the next rebellion. What no one outside that pirate fleet knew was that the specters only wore the guise of pirates to accumulate resources and wealth for what they truly were...

Torrents.

The *Gryphon*—a small and agile gunship left over from the Uprising—was the first non-pirate ship to become part of the torrent fleet, but it wasn't the last. The next ship added to the fleet—the fleet's ace card—sat not far from the *Gryphon* and *Honorless*, but no one could see it even if they tried. Unlike the other ships in the fleet, that one had stealth capabilities. Not only could it run silently, but it could also run invisibly. Without the newest addition to the fleet, Reyne wouldn't even have considered trapping a CUF ship.

"Surprise," Throttle said. "All systems checks ran clean. Again."

"No kidding," Sixx added. "All weapons checks ran clean. Again."

Reyne didn't respond. Instead, he leaned forward to better

see his panel. A red blip had appeared on the edge of the grid near the wide opening of the funnel, where the two smallest ships in Critch's fleet waited more than a thousand clicks out from each other. "Looks like we're about to find out if our mousetrap will work. Throttle, throw the shields up and cycle the nav engines."

"Shields are up. Cycling engines now," she confirmed.

"Good," Reyne said. "Sixx, open the gun bays and power up the guns."

"How about the cannon?"

He considered it for a moment. "Better power it up to be safe."

Sixx clapped his hands together. "Finally."

Reyne spun his seat around and pointed at the other man. "Remember, the cannon is a last resort. You don't fire it unless we have no other option. The last thing we want to do is blow up our payload."

"Yeah, yeah, I got it."

"They haven't changed course or speed," Throttle said. "So far, so good."

The CUF ship about to enter the funnel was limping back to the main fleet at sub-speed. Unknown to the crew on board, its jump engines had failed courtesy of sabotage by a low-level fringe conscript who'd been more than happy to help out the torrent cause...for a price, of course.

Reyne watched the large blip as it approached their trap. It had taken over a month to prepare for this mission, and they had no backup plan if they failed. The risks involved had given Reyne heartburn every night for the past week. Worse, not sleeping well made his joints ache worse, and he found he was going through twice as many painkillers as usual.

He watched the blip fly between the first two yellow circles without changing course. As it progressed between the second pair, his confidence grew and he found himself breathing easier.

"They're coming straight in. Won't be much longer before their comms are jammed."

Jamming tech was highly illegal, and a favorite trick of pirates since it was undetectable until a ship tried to make or receive a transmission. Crews often thought their systems were malfunctioning, and by the time they figured out they were being attacked, the pirates had latched on to their ship.

The *Gryphon* was the only ship in the torrent fleet not yet upgraded with jamming tech, but the *Honorless* was close enough to cover the full narrow end of the funnel trap. As the CUF ship moved into the funnel, the ships farthest out began to close in behind it, shutting off retreat routes and ensuring it remained jammed from all directions.

Jamming tech, however, had two problems. One problem was that it sucked power and could drain a ship's reserves in no time flat. The other problem was that it was short-range. The entire fleet needed to use jamming comms, hitting the supply ship simultaneously from every direction, with the hope that by working together they would generate enough static to smother the incoming ship's transmissions.

The *Matador* was part of the Collective Unified Forces' largest class of supply ships. It was massive, large enough to hold three warships within its storage tanks. The CUF ship would be on its own against the torrent fleet, but was in no way an underdog. The *Matador* outgunned them all...with the exception of their ace card.

If the *Matador* got any transmissions through, the torrent fleet ran the risk of facing a battle they could never win. While all the torrent ships had their own guns, they would do little damage against a warship, let alone the multiple warships Corps General Ausyar would send if he found out where the torrents were. Ausyar had been scouring the Collective for Reyne and Critch for the past year. The leader of the CUF had voiced, on all the Collective news channels his vow to take down the torrents, and he'd been doing his best to track them down since then. After a year of running and hiding, the torrents were finally ready to make their next move.

As their target moved deeper into the funnel, Reyne looked out the view panel to get a visual on their target. It didn't take long. The huge round gray ship cut through space like a fat Alluvian bass through water. He gulped at the sight of the beast approaching them.

A flicker in the black drew his gaze. The largest ship in the torrent fleet—the *Arcadia*—blinked into view.

"What are they doing out of stealth?" Reyne asked. "The fleet's not in place yet."

The *Matador* slowed. Reyne suspected they were trying to communicate with what they believed to be another CUF ship, only to discover that their comms weren't working.

Warnings flashed across his panel, indicating their target had figured out the threat far more quickly than most and was responding by powering up its shields and opening its weapon systems.

"Looks like they're realized it's the *Arcadia* and not one of theirs," Reyne announced. "Prepare for evasive maneuvers."

The *Arcadia* fired a warning shot across the *Matador*'s bow, and the CUF ship responded by firing dozens of photon shots in all directions.

Throttle banked the ship hard in hope to miss a blinding shot.

"It looks like they've located all of us."

"Fire back?" Sixx asked.

"Not yet," Reyne said. "We don't want to rile them up too much."

"They're already shooting at us. How much more riled up can they get?"

The *Matador* fired again. This time, Throttle pulled up and snap-rolled the *Gryphon*. The force of the blast sent a shudder through the hull.

"I lost gun Five," Sixx announced.

"Nav engine two isn't responding," Throttle added.

Sixx looked up. "On the bright side, if they'd used cannons, we'd be dead already."

A rotating red beacon below the *Arcadia* alerted Reyne. "It's safe to say we're switching to Plan B."

While the *Matador* was bigger, the *Arcadia* was a warship, carrying many times more the armament and weaponry as the supply ship. One of those weapons was an EMP engine. There was no visible sign of the weapon being fired—EMPs were invisible to the human eye—but the results couldn't be missed. Lights across the ship's hull went dark as though someone flipped a switch.

For an interminable minute, the *Matador* faced the *Arcadia* in a deadly staring contest to see who would blink first.

Throttle broke the silence. "We're lucky that ship doesn't have an EMP shield."

Reyne grimaced. "Unfortunately, there's a reason Plan B wasn't Plan A. If we can secure the *Matador*'s crew, that ship is still going to be out of commission until we can recycle the electrical systems. Bringing a ship that size back online could take several hours."

Throttle shrugged. "Since they didn't get off any distress calls before we hit them, we shouldn't have anything to worry about. We should have it up and running and be long gone before the CUF sends a search-and-rescue patrol."

"I know, but I don't like being stuck on its flight path longer than we have to."

Three transport ships emerged from the *Arcadia*'s docking bays and headed over to the surrounded supply ship. "Phase Two is on," Reyne announced. "Let's hope the CUF crew surrenders peacefully instead of doing something stupid."

"I bet there's plenty of adrenaline-laced terror buzzing through that crew right about now," Sixx said.

Reyne nodded, and worried for the teams docking on the *Matador*. He'd served as a chaser when he was conscripted into the CUF, and had been on more than his share of missions like this, where a little mistake could result in disaster. The *Arcadia* had its cannons leveled at the supply ship, and he hoped the threat would be enough for the CUF crew to know they'd been beaten and to surrender peacefully. Unfortunately, asking them to surrender wasn't easy when comms were being jammed.

Anxiety caused his joints to ache. He didn't move, not until four long minutes later, when the *Matador*'s outer lights flashed the all clear in Morse code.

Reyne relaxed. "Light us up, Throttle." He tapped his comm. "The *Matador* is down, and the *Arcadia* is now securing the crew. You okay back there, Boden?"

"Got nailed in the shin by a wrench."

Throttle's eyes widened. "Are you okay?"

"Yeah, I'm fine. The ship got a bit rattled, and I'm showing some minor damage to the hull and photon gun five."

"Can we still make jump speed if we need to?"

"We don't have the juice to make jump speed," Throttle interrupted, and Reyne silenced her by holding up his hand.

"Yes. I'm showing no loss of integrity to the jump shields or to the engines, but the aft nav engine system needs to be recycled. The earliest we could jump is fifteen minutes."

"Throttle will recycle the system up here."

A second later, Reyne's message channel lit up. He opened it to find a broadcast from Critch:

Honorless: Tango is reported secure. Maintain jams until tango is visually verified. Report status on this data channel.

. . .

Reyne typed a response. By the time he finished, other responses had already begun to light up the screen.

Lady Lilith: No damage.

Nighthawk: Engine running hot. Running scans. Will check back if need help.

Gryphon: Rattled from blast echo. Recycling nav engines.

Winter Wind: Damage to both nav engines and jump shield is down. We can limp around but need to dock for repairs.

Arcadia: Winter Wind, dock at bay Seven.

Winter Wind: Arcadia, wilco.

Scorpia: No damage.

Maelstrom: No damage. That was one hell of a show.

Mustang Run: Suffered hull breach. We've patched it for now, but it's not going to hold. We need to dock immediately.

Honorless: Scorpia, shadow Mustang in case she needs to move crew.

Scorpia: Mustang, on our way.

Arcadia: Mustang Run, proceed to docking bay Six.

Night Velvet: No damage.

Mustang Run: Arcadia, negative. Need a tow. NOW.

Delilah: No damage.

Scorpia: Mustang, prepare for tow hooks. Coming up alongside now.

Ocelot: No damage, though Roq needs to change his pants.

SkyE Rider: No damage. Ginger Grey lost her comms and primary systems, but we have visual Morse confirmation that she's otherwise in good shape.

Crazy's Coral: No damage worth reporting.

Blue Jay: No damage. Thirsty for juice.

Honorless: Rainmaker, report.

.

.

Maelstrom: Have visual of debris. Looks like we lost Rainmaker.

HONORLESS: Maelstrom, verify.

.

.

.

MAELSTROM: Rainmaker took a direct hit. Hull is fully breached. Will send out a search party, but it doesn't look good.

HONORLESS: Maelstrom, search for survivors. Everyone else, proceed to tango to verify crew and ship is secure.

.

.

ARCADIA: We have secured all operational areas of the Matador. It is now safe to disable transmission dampeners and switch to broadcast network.

As the radios came alive, Reyne's lips thinned. "We lost *Rainmaker*. Robo's crew is searching for survivors."

"*Rainmaker?* Wasn't that Geena's ship?" Sixx asked, frowning.

Reyne nodded. "Yeah. She had four crew members. All of them were from Spate."

Sixx grimaced. "Pity. She was a hell of a cage fighter. First woman to nearly beat me in the cage."

"She beat you?"

"I said *nearly* beat me."

After a long moment of silence, Sixx continued. "Losing a ship is rough, but you have to admit those losses are low considering we went up against a CUF ship."

Reyne nodded and sighed. "Throttle, get the *Gryphon* ready

to dock on the *Matador*. Everyone's coming in to make sure the ship and her crew are secure. Then, we'll refuel."

"Good. We're practically running on fumes."

"If Heid's intel on what the *Matador*'s carrying is good, we'll have enough juice to keep the fleet flying at jump speeds for a year," Reyne said.

Ships could run off solar sails indefinitely, but when your enemies had jump speed, you needed jump speed. And going that fast burned juice.

A light blinked on his panel. "Ah, hell. They must've had some EMP-shielded systems. They just fired off a distress call. We're going to have company."

CHAPTER 2

HUNTING PARTY

"THIS IS THE ARCADIA. *We have encountered pockets of resistance during suppression activities. At least one distress call has been broadcast from an unknown location on board the* Matador. *We request immediate support in searching the craft and neutralizing remaining threats post haste."*

"Sounds like I'd better grab my gear," Sixx said.

"Good plan." Reyne checked the photon pistol holstered on his thigh, while Sixx unbuckled from his seat and headed from the bridge.

"You heard 'em, specters," Critch's voice broadcast over the network. *"Get on that ship and find the assholes jeopardizing our juice run. Once you're on board the* Matador, *use comm frequency three-five-six-eight. And fire up those viggin' jammers again so our tango can't get an RSVP back from their pals."*

"I can have us docked in no time," Throttle said.

Reyne felt a surge in the ship's speed. He reached for the comm and eyed Throttle as he pinged the *Gryphon*'s mechanic. "Boden, we're docking at the *Matador*, which is mostly under control. Sixx and I are going on board. I need you and Throttle to stay back to refuel and fix us up for jump speed. I have a feeling we're not going to have much time to hang around and socialize before our CUF buddies show up."

"What do you mean by 'mostly under control'?" came Boden's reply.

Reyne answered, "You'd better plan on expecting trouble."

"I always do."

"How soon do you think the CUF will respond?" Throttle asked.

He shrugged. "It depends on how close their nearest ship is. Could be ten hours, could be ten minutes."

She stiffened. "Let's hope it's ten hours."

Throttle had the *Gryphon* docked at the *Matador* in less than five minutes, latching on to one of the supply ship's twenty or so docking tubes. Reyne and Sixx bypassed the decon chamber and jogged into a massive hallway, where they met the heavily scarred Critch along with the slim Birk and the roughhewn Chutt, who'd entered the hallway at roughly the same time.

While the large hallway was noticeably smaller than those on warships, the floors and walls were the same drab tan color that the interiors of all CUF ships were painted with. As they turned a corner, Reyne found an ex-dromadier from the *Arcadia* standing guard while several of her counterparts escorted the CUF crew into an escape pod. She turned as Reyne's group approached, and rushed to meet them.

Critch stomped up to her. "What was that stunt your captain pulled out there—dropping out of stealth early?"

She cowered under his glare. "Stealth burned up the last of our juice faster than projected. We were forced to drop out."

Critch glared. The scars that crisscrossed his face whitened and puckered more than usual. "That miscalculation cost me a good ship and five souls."

The guard swallowed. "There was nothing we could do—"

"We'll have plenty of time to debrief later," Reyne interrupted. "Now, I need you to give us the current situation. What are we up against?"

"We've verified the bridge is fully secure," the woman replied, looking relieved to no longer be under Critch's scrutinizing glare. "Same with the engine room. Those are the only two locations with known long-range comms. We're running scans for portables, but it's a big ship and our numbers are thin. We've only had a chance to perform cursory checks through the crew quarters and central holds so far."

She continued. "Since your ships are jamming their comms, we've switched focus back to our original plan. We've nearly completed the decoupling of the systems from central CUF Command so they can't take remote control of the ship. As soon as we're done with that, we'll reboot the systems and plug in jump coordinates." She motioned to the *Matador*'s crew. "We're also prepping the crew for loading into the escape pods."

"Obviously not the *entire* crew, or else we wouldn't be having to divide our numbers to hunt when we need to be refueling and making jump speed with our prize," Critch argued.

She bristled. "Captain Heid would send over more support if she could, but she needs as many hands as she can retain on board to hold off any CUF ships that arrive."

"I'd much rather we are all out of here long before they arrive," Reyne said.

Critch glanced down the hallway. "My team will start in the crew quarters. Some rich techie could have a portable long-range comm in his room."

"Sixx and I will work our way through the hold," Reyne said.

The soldier pointed down the hallway. "The elevator is straight ahead, but the power grid is still down, so you'll have to take the stairs next to it. Crew quarters are one level up on Nine.

The cargo holds can be accessed from all the even-numbered levels. Just turn left at the elevator, and you'll see the entrance."

"Keep an eye out for the remaining crews as they dock," Critch said. "Route them as they arrive to spread out coverage. We have to neutralize this threat before we make jump speed or else we could be leaving breadcrumbs all the way back to base. You have the comm channel to report anything."

"Yes, captain," she replied.

The five men headed down the halls.

"Move fast," Reyne cautioned. "Who knows how much time we have before these guys' pals show up."

"You do the same," Critch replied as he shoved open the door to the stairwell.

As Critch and his team disappeared up the stairs, Reyne and Sixx made a left and came to a set of double doors. The entrance had no windows, so there was no way to see what lay on the other side. He tossed a quick glance in Sixx's direction to find the other man already had a pistol in his hand.

"Let's go hunting," Sixx said, sounding much more nonchalant than Reyne felt.

Reyne drew his pistol and pulled open the door.

The younger man stepped through first, sweeping the immediate area with a broad movement. Reyne followed through to stand at Sixx's side.

They stood in an open-framed hallway that encircled the massive storage area. The tank for zero-g refueling filled the central space, Pallets of supplies and modular workrooms took up the surrounding perimeter. Unlike the *Gryphon*, which had crates lining every open centimeter of wall space, most of these walls were bare—evidently, the CUF didn't have to worry about efficiently using open space.

"There are too many places to hide around here." Sixx

motioned to the levels of open hallways and stairs. "Too easy to see someone coming."

Too easy to take someone down with a single shot, Reyne thought to himself, but said instead, "It's safe to say that if anyone's in here, they're watching us as we speak. Let's keep moving. Start on one end and work our way around the tank, and keep eyes on the exits at all times."

Sixx acknowledged with a nod, and took the lead. They moved quickly to the stairs and headed down eight flights to the landing below.

The gravity on the ship was greater than the point seven gravity he kept the EM generators at on the *Gryphon*, and the increased stress echoed through his arthritic joints with each step. He missed the last rung and landed hard with a grunt. Embarrassed, he straightened and washed the wince from his face. Fortunately, Sixx hadn't noticed, or at least wasn't in the mood to heckle him about his age.

As his partner weaved fluidly around pallets, Reyne made a mental note to use the gravity booth more often to help combat the arthritis he'd acquired from too many years spent in low gravity.

Sixx paused to peer into a small workroom before continuing onward. He led the way across the floor, slowly and steadily, checking out every pallet and workroom. He came to a hard stop in the doorway of a larger workroom. "Well, hello, gorgeous."

Reyne followed his friend into the room, his weapon raised. When he saw what the other man had seen, he relaxed and smiled. Heid's intel was spot-on, making the entire mission worth the risk. "You're right. She sure is gorgeous."

Before them was a black rilon device that stood ten meters tall and ten meters wide. The back end was small—not much more than a panel for entering design inputs. The front end was easily fifteen feet wide, the largest Reyne had ever seen on a 3D printer. With access to the right source material, they could print any part imaginable.

After the Uprising, 3D printers had been outlawed for private ownership because they had made it too easy for the torrents to produce their own weapons. Though, the bigger reason may have been that the Collective didn't like not being able to make a profit off anything the fringe produced for itself.

"If she would fit on the *Gryphon*," Sixx began, "I'd be hooking her up to the crane and moving her on board this very minute."

Reyne's lips parted. "The crane."

"I was joking. Sort of. But if you're all for trying it, I'm in. I'm just not sure we'll be able to get it moved over before the rest of the CUF is up our tailpipes."

Reyne thumped his head. "I should've thought of it before. On most ships, the bridge is the only location with external comm panels."

"Yeah, so?"

"Except on supply ships, the boom operators need external comms so they can resupply the ship when it's still at central docks, before the crew comes back on aboard."

Sixx's gaze shot outside the workroom. "We need to get to that crane."

They bypassed searching any remaining pallets and workrooms, and hustled to make their way around the gigantic fuel tank and closer to the ship's crane. As they jogged, they were careful to stay within the tank's shadow for cover.

Reaching the crane proved to be a bit more of a challenge than Reyne had anticipated. He'd expected to see the crane above him with a metal stair going straight up to it. Instead, the machine was built into the far wall with no visible ladder.

"I've got movement in the box," Sixx said.

"How many?"

"Just caught a glimpse. At least one, but could be more."

Reyne counted from the floor up to the level where the crane was built nearly flush into the wall. The boom was locked in against the wall below it. They could climb the boom, but it didn't look easy.

He hit his personal locator beacon. He spoke softly into his comm. "This is Reyne and Sixx in the central holds. We've located the likely source of the distress call. One—possibly more—drom is holed up in the crane. We can get to them from the hold, but it sure would be nice to have someone cut off their escape route on level Four, directly above my current position. Are there any teams in the area?"

"This is Critch. We're moving into position right now."

"Don't go in," Reyne added. "Not until you get my signal."

No response.

"You know he won't wait," Sixx said.

"I know." He motioned to the boom. "Better start climbing."

Sixx climbed the boom quickly and easily, while Reyne struggled. He pulled himself up, climbing in smaller increments. If Critch tried to break through the crane's door, chances were the dromadier would try to escape out the front—right into Sixx's and Reyne's arms, which would likely cause a deadly fall for anyone involved.

If the guy managed to escape without getting anyone killed, then Sixx and Reyne would end up having to chase him around the holds. They didn't have the time, and Reyne certainly didn't have the endurance.

Adrenaline helped him climb faster to reach the box before Critch's team.

Sixx had nearly reached the top when an explosion blew out the crane's windows. Reyne lowered his face just before shards of clear plastic pelted him.

"Damn it, Critch," Reyne muttered as he brushed plastic pieces off his shoulders.

Above him, Sixx leapt into the box, and he hustled to catch up. He could hear the ensuing scuffle as he climbed. By the time he reached the window ledge, the crane room had fallen silent. He found Sixx holding a single dromadier in a chokehold. Critch stood facing them between Birk and Chutt, who had their pistols aimed at the prisoner.

"Sending a message out to CUF Command wasn't a smart idea," Reyne heard Critch say as he climbed over the ledge.

The dromadier's chin jutted outward. "I was doing my duty."

"You're a fool if you think you're serving the Collective."

"Better the Collective than filthy scum like you," the man retorted.

Critch smiled. "You know the whole 'don't shoot the messenger' thing?"

The man's gaze narrowed. "Uh, yeah."

Reyne pushed to his feet, a rock forming in his gut. "Critch, don't..."

Critch unholstered his pistol. "You see, I've never abided by that philosophy." He shot the dromadier.

Sixx dropped the man and stared wide-eyed at Critch. "You could've hit me, you damn pirate."

Critch ignored him as he holstered his pistol.

Sixx continued. "A little warning next time would be nice."

Chutt gave a toothy grin. "Quit complaining. You didn't get shot, you pansy."

Sixx's lips thinned and he took a step toward Chutt.

"Bring it on," Chutt said, still smiling.

"Enough!" Reyne turned a hard glare onto Critch. "That kid didn't have to die. Sixx had him under control. He posed no risk to us."

Critch strolled over to the comm panel and spoke without

making eye contact. "The rest of the crew is already loaded onto escape pods, and none of us have the resources to take care of a prisoner in our brigs."

"The *Arcadia* could've taken him."

"You know as well as I do we don't have the time right now to deal with loose ends."

Reyne glowered for a long moment, his jaw clenched.

Critch typed several commands, then looked up. "He was only able to fire off the one message, though one was enough. I've locked this panel. No one's sending anything else from here without hacking through my protocols."

"*Attention, specters,*" a male voice came over everyone's wrist comms. "*We are tracking incoming ships on jump speed. Estimated time of arrival is eight minutes.*"

"Well, that's faster than I expected," Critch said before tapping his comm, and his voice broadcast on all comms. "Initiate Scatter immediately. You know the drill. If you're not where you need to be, then you'd better get there. All ships better be ready for jump speed in five minutes."

Reyne motioned to Sixx before telling Critch and his crew, "We'll talk about this later."

"You know I did the right thing. We're already dealing with too many risks. We can't afford a prisoner escaping our base and reporting back to Ausyar."

"I know," Reyne said quietly. He paused at the doorway. "Good luck with Seda."

Critch grunted. "I think you'll need more than luck with Lincoln. Watch yourself."

Reyne gave a small nod. He and Sixx jogged from the room and back toward the *Gryphon*. On the way there, he pinged Throttle. "We're on our way back to you. What's your status?"

"*We don't have time to finish refueling, so juice is only at forty-six percent. Still, that's enough to make jump speed a few times. Boden has given the thumbs up on the hull and systems, so we're good to go as soon as you slackers get back here,"* she reported.

"Good," Reyne said. "Start up the engines. We'll be there in under two minutes."

"ETA of incoming traffic is six minutes," the same male voice from the earlier broadcast returned.

Reyne ran as fast as he could, and Sixx easily kept pace next to him. They met a couple other torrent crews running to their own ships. The pair sprinted through the docking tube, and Reyne hit the switch to disconnect from the tube the instant the *Gryphon's* door closed and the pressurization seal flashed green.

"Sixx, take the guns. Throttle, take us out," Reyne said as he entered the bridge.

"Buckle in," Throttle said. "I'm pulling out of the dock now."

"ETA of incoming traffic is four minutes."

Reyne strapped in and pulled up the grid. "Keep an eye on your nine o'clock, Throttle. It looks like the *Nighthawk* is trying to cut into our personal space."

"I've got them," she answered as she continued to reverse the *Gryphon* from the dock. The *Nighthawk* also continued to back up, moving closer and closer to the *Gryphon*. Throttle spun her ship around, missing the other ship while pulling farther from the *Matador*. "Lemmy sure could use some flying lessons," she muttered.

Sixx snickered. "I hear Lemmy has been asking you for some private lessons."

Throttle rolled her eyes. "I'll hand it to him. He's persistent."

"ETA of incoming traffic is two minutes. All ships make jump speed post haste. The Arcadia will not remain to provide support."

"The jump engine is just about at full power," she said.

Reyne pinged Boden. "Prepare for jump speed."

"I'm strapped in and ready back here," Boden answered.

"Get us into jump speed the instant you see the *Matador* jump, but don't wait until our timer is gone," Reyne ordered. "I really don't want to be here when the CUF shows up and blasts the area with an EMP net."

He noticed two blips disappear from the grid as other ships made jump speed. Outside the window, he watched an escape pod shoot from the *Matador* and its docking doors close. "Hurry up," he muttered. As more ships jumped, soon all that remained was the *Matador,* the *Arcadia,* the *Honorless,* and the *Gryphon.*

Seconds later, the supply ship accelerated briefly and then shot forward, disappearing in a burst of light. "They're clear," Reyne said. "Get us out of here, Throttle."

The *Arcadia* jumped next, and he noticed the *Honorless* accelerate at the same time the *Gryphon* moved. Just as he was thrown back in his seat, he caught several flashes of CUF ships emerging from jump speed.

The *Gryphon* jumped, and Reyne lost all visuals. He slumped over his panel and sighed.

"That was close," Throttle exclaimed.

Sixx added, "We're now the proud owners of a fully loaded supply ship with a mighty fine 3D printer. Think of all the different kinds of mayhem we can make now."

A rock formed in Reyne's gut as he thought of how close they'd come to being caught. They'd survived the past year by lying low and steering far from any CUF ships. Beginning today, their plans had shifted. A year of running had burned through the fleet's fuel supply, and they were running out of places to dock for repairs and food. They couldn't take on the Collective when they were constantly on the run.

And so it was time for them to take action.

Corps General Ausyar and the CUF armada were about to have their hands full.

CHAPTER 3

SCATTER PLOT

THROTTLE SCRUNCHED HER NOSE. "I don't like Devil Town. It's full of criminals."

"Which is why we'll fit right in," Sixx said.

She frowned. "You act like it's no big deal. You've had a price on your head since you were fourteen. It's still relatively new to me."

He shot the pilot a toothy grin. "Trust me. Guys love a dangerous woman."

The petite blonde rolled her eyes. "Anyone ever tell you you're hopeless?"

"Yup," he replied before taking a long drink and then added, "Don't worry. You're staying on the ship with Boden."

"You don't think he'll try to buy sweet soy while we're down there, do you?"

Sixx shrugged. "Once an addict, always an addict."

"Hm. Some could say the same about you with women," she countered.

"It's different. I enjoy the company of beautiful women to remember. Addicts use drugs to forget."

"Oh, so you're a philosopher now, too?"

Reyne ate his dinner, listening to the pair as they bantered, letting the normalcy soothe his nerves. Sixx and Throttle were both more than crew; they were family. He'd found his adopted daughter at the end of the Uprising over twenty years ago. She'd been only a few years old when he came across her at a ravaged farm, lying next to her dead family. Her broken spine would've guaranteed her death within hours or days.

He'd seen too much death—*had caused* too much death—by the time he found her. He'd grown numb to killing. Yet, her tiny grip had brought him back from the blackness into which his soul had comfortably settled. She'd always believed he'd saved her, but the truth was that she'd saved him that day. And she'd been in his heart and a member of the *Gryphon*'s crew ever since.

Sixx joined his crew nearly ten years ago. Reyne had come across the thief at Sol Base, holding his own against a dozen armed thugs. Reyne had planned to continue along his way, but there'd been something about Sixx's dark gaze that'd brought Reyne right back to the day he'd found Throttle, when he too had been a lost man about to tumble into the abyss.

He later learned that Sixx had lost his wife a few months earlier and had developed reckless and dangerous habits to cope. Reyne, seeing his old self in Sixx, stepped into a matter that didn't concern him. He helped Sixx escape some rich woman's irate husband and his posse, and ended up with a new crew member. He quickly learned that Sixx's masculine features and killer charm made him irresistible to women...and made for all kinds of new and interesting trouble.

"Well, we're torrents, not criminals," Throttle said. "Big difference. One is heroic; the other is vile."

Sixx shrugged. "Both are one and the same to the CUF."

Reyne chimed in. "Keep in mind that we have the two most powerful men in the Collective out to get us. Everyone knows if you want to find people bad enough, put out a big reward on their heads, big enough that even their own mothers will turn them in. Whether we're criminals or not is a moot point."

Sixx chuckled. "Which makes our mission all the more interesting, since of course we're heading straight to a fringe station where there's guaranteed to be patrols around every corner."

Reyne lifted a brow. "Would you prefer we give up and return to Playa?"

"Heck, no. Just thinking of the temperatures at Tulan Base makes my balls freeze."

Throttle winced. "Gross. That's an image that will haunt me forever."

"Spate is definitely warmer," Reyne said.

Sixx grinned. "And the women are feistier."

Throttle smirked. "We've been away for a long time. What if your girlfriends forgot about you?"

"Nah. I'm unforgettable. I just hope they didn't get too lonely while I've been gone. I don't want them to get too overzealous when they see me."

"If things don't go well, I'm afraid you won't get much time to catch up," Reyne said. "It only takes one scout to see us and our mission is scrubbed. If that happens, we'll have to cut tail and rendezvous with the others back at Tulan Base to come up with a new plan...while your balls freeze off."

Sixx dramatically shivered. "That's all the motivation I need to make sure this goes off without a hitch."

"We could always meet up with Critch on Terra," Throttle offered.

Reyne belted out a humorless laugh. "My presence on Terra would do far more harm than good. No, with the specters scattered across the fringe to recruit, we stick with the plans."

Throttle leaned forward. "Do you think Heid got the *Matador* safely to Playa?"

"I do," Reyne said. "The Collective has always underestimated Playa. It might be a big ice rock, but it still has plenty of natural resources, like the metals used to produce rilon. Even after the Collective destroyed Ice Port, there are still plenty of factories in the smaller towns. I know the colonists still on Playa are more than willing to reopen the factories in exchange for food and resources."

"Assuming Heid is able to negotiate with the locals," Sixx said. "Playans are known to be a rather standoffish group."

"She'll do it," Throttle said with confidence. "She might be an Alluvian, but she's as tough as a Playan and doesn't understand the meaning of the word no. She'll have the production lines running at a hundred percent in weeks."

"The bigger problem will be hiding the *Arcadia* and the *Matador* from the CUF surveillance drones in orbit around Playa," Reyne said.

"Nah," Sixx said. "She's got a warship. They have all kinds of techy gadgets to screw with drones' tracking systems."

"If Ausyar sees even a hint of activity taking place on Playa, you can bet he'll fill the planet's orbit with warships," Reyne cautioned. "It's safe to say none of us have any interest in running into Ausyar's *Trinity*—or any warships for that matter, not with us topping the CUF's most-wanted list right now."

"No thanks to you," Sixx said. "I was there, remember?"

Reyne's lips thinned. He remembered quite well. The night they broke into a Myrad mansion, killing the owner—who happened to be Ausyar's lover—by accident.

Throttle scowled. "Ausyar left the Playans to starve after he bombed Ice Port. We should return the favor to his home world, Myr. I heard Critch still has his hands on the blight they used on Sol Base last year."

"We don't attack innocents," Reyne said. "We'll win our freedom without stooping to Ausyar's level." He leaned back in his chair. "Phase One was a success. With the *Matador*'s 3D printer brought down to Playa's surface, we can print all the munitions and hardware we need and store it beneath Tulan Base. It's more efficient than bundling the rilon for interstellar transport and then printing it into supplies."

Sixx ran a hand through his black hair. "Yeah, that's all good and fine, but we're still printing magnetic rifles, which went obsolete over a century ago. We'll be going up against the CUF, and they have photon guns. We might as well print rubber bands to shoot at them."

"Photon guns are too expensive and complicated to make. Magnetic technology may be old, but it's reliable and gets the job done."

"I think ramping up Tulan Base as our main base is a fantastic plan," Throttle said.

"Of course you do. It was your dad's idea," Sixx replied drily.

"He doesn't always have good ideas," she corrected him before turning to Reyne. "Like the time you left me behind last year to go traipsing off to Myr and Alluvia. That was a horrible idea. You guys just about got yourselves killed. Remember who had to come and save the day?"

"You did," Reyne answered.

"She makes a good point," Sixx said. "That was an awful idea. We nearly all died, and I didn't even get to keep any of the goodies I found on Myr."

"You still have that biome kit you found on that Myrad hauler, right?"

"Yeah, but that's all for me. The stuff I was grabbing on Myr was for bartering."

"Who knows, maybe you'll get another chance to tour Myr," Reyne said.

Sixx steepled his fingers and his lips curled upward. "I like the sound of that."

Reyne smiled. "Did I tell you another fantastic idea I had?"

Throttle narrowed her gaze. "What's that?"

"Heid isn't just producing munitions. She's also stripping hardware from the *Matador* to fortify Tulan Base and expand the space dock."

Throttle's eyes widened. "Expanding the dock? Heid might be my new favorite person."

"It was my idea," Reyne said.

A chime interrupted them.

Reyne looked up. "We'll be dropping out of jump speed soon. Let's hope our ship's new credentials get us through security, or else we've come a long way just to get shot at. Again."

"I guess that means I have to get back to work." Throttle pushed her wheelchair back from the table and headed to the bridge.

Sixx collected the food trays. "The specters have been making up false credentials for twenty years. They'll work just fine."

"I'm counting on it." Reyne left the cleaning to Sixx and caught up with Throttle on the bridge, where she was locking her wheelchair in at her instrument panel. He took a seat at his own panel to her left.

The *Gryphon* was a Phantom III class gunship, and had been Reyne's personal ship during the Uprising. While her technology was over twenty years old, she made up for it with speed and armament. With a Flux Whisper engine, she could outrun any ship below the Aggressor class. Plus, having been retrofitted with a phase cannon and five photon guns came in handy when they couldn't outrun their problems.

He heard Sixx buckle in at the gunner's station behind him. If luck were on their side, they wouldn't have to use her speed or her guns on this mission. As Reyne ran scans, he hoped for luck, but knew it was always better to prepare for the worst.

Throttle broadcast to the engine room. "Heads up, Boden. We're dropping out of jump speed in three, two, one."

The constant hum of the Flux engine disappeared, leaving the ship in sudden silence.

"I'm switching to navigational engines," Throttle announced.

A moment later, Boden's voice came through. *"Everything's in the green back here."*

A small brown planet grew larger through the view panel. Reyne scanned the channels, not picking up any chatter out of the ordinary. "Transmitting codes to the station now." Running his hands over the panel, he transmitted the clearance codes and ship data. Then, he waited.

Long seconds passed before his panel chimed a response. He accepted the files and let out the breath he'd been holding. "We've been cleared for approach and have a vector. So far, so good."

"Adjusting course heading now," Throttle said.

In zero-g, the only indication that Throttle was changing course was the slight shift of Spate standing before them in the view panel. Getting used to the nuances of zero-g had been Reyne's longest learning curve when he was a new pilot. Since the only gravity on board came from the ship's electromagnetic fields, the crew didn't feel shifts or g-force. Only when a ship moved from sub-speed to jump speed was there noticeable thrust, and that was due to the slight delay in the EM fields adjusting to the engine's surge.

As they approached Spate, light twinkled off ships and satellites circling in the planet's orbit. Reyne couldn't make out which ships were CUF patrols and which were haulers or transports, but he knew the Collective was closely guarding all the fringe stations. After all, the fringe stations were the only colonies on each fringe world with space docks. And most ships, including the *Gryphon*, weren't designed to take off from gravity-worlds without external propulsion systems, which space docks provided.

As Spate loomed ever closer, Devil Town—the planet's only fringe station—came into view. Even this far out, its massive domed gardens stood out like green ribbons draping across the colony.

His panel beeped, feeding the ship additional information. "Looks like our credentials were accepted. We're cleared for landing at dock C-Five."

"I'm pulling up docking bay C's layout now," Throttle said.

"I'm not seeing any patrols closing in on us," Sixx said. "That's always a good sign."

When the dark gray docking station came into view, Throttle began reciting her landing checklist, a habit she'd picked up when she'd first started flying at the age of five. When she finished, she blew out a breath. "Devil Town, here we come."

CHAPTER 4

FROZEN DREAMS

"EXCUSE ME, captain? Where do I put these?"

Gabriela Heid turned to find a young man with his arms full of cables. "What are they?"

"Power couplers from the *Matador*," he answered succinctly.

"Take them to Nolin at the slingshot systems," she said. "Maybe he can use them."

When the man moved on, another took his place. "I have a new tribe of Playans at the gate. Where can I put them?"

"See if there's still room on level Three."

"Level Three is already over capacity."

She sighed. "Start using the warehouse space on level Two then."

"It's freezing on that level."

"They're Playans. It'll be far warmer than what they've just come in from. Give them extra blankets and food. That should help."

Nolin came jogging up. "I can't work on these systems. They're older than I am."

Heid gripped his shoulder. "Please, just try."

He frowned and then nodded tightly. "Okay."

"Thank you," she said, forcing a thin smile and turning away. She walked down the hall. When she saw more headed her way, she sprung around the corner and found a dark nook. She slid down the wall. She rested her throbbing head on her knees and rubbed her neck.

A year ago, she was a senior CUF officer in charge of one of the armada's newest warships. Back then, she never would've imagined that in just one year, she'd have run off with her warship, hijacked a CUF supply ship, set up a torrent base on a fringe world, and betrayed her father. She was the highest profile citizen traitor to the Collective, and number one on the CUF's most-wanted list, but that didn't bother her nearly as much as knowing her father was on the hunt for her.

Gabriel Heid was Alluvia's highest-ranking magistrate. What only a very elite few knew was that he was also known as Mason, one of the three leaders of the Founders. He was a brilliant man who'd become the most powerful man in the Collective by pulling strings and working deals behind the scenes. He touted that his aims were altruistic, but his actions showed his motives to be far different.

She'd watched as he morphed the Founders into a clandestine organization serving his own needs rather than the needs of the Collective. He could design intricate strategies for shaping the Collective, and incorporate a multitude of variables into those strategies. However, the one variable that he'd taken for granted was that his daughter would always follow him, without question. When she'd betrayed him, she knew she would draw the full depths of his vengeance.

The other Founders also sought vengeance for her betrayal of them, but she didn't see her actions as betrayal. The secret organization had been established to ensure power was distributed equally across the Collective, yet much of what they were doing was only preserving the unfair authority Myr and Alluvia held over the Collective's remaining four planets in the fringe. Every action she'd taken was to work toward the Founders' initial goal, though she suspected she was on borrowed time. Because if there was one thing the Founders excelled at, it was removing anyone deemed a risk to their plans.

For now, she hid where Mason's spies couldn't reach her. But she couldn't remain in hiding forever. At some point she'd have to face her demon, and a part of her looked forward to that day. He had trained her to be strong and relentless, and she planned to show him that she'd learned her lessons well.

First things first.

The torrents needed her more than she needed to stop Mason. Once Tulan Base was running at full capacity, then she could focus on taking her father down, slice by slice.

"There you are."

Heid looked up to find Sylvian, a tech who served on the *Arcadia*'s command deck. Heid smiled weakly and raised her hands in surrender. "You found me."

"I have a few forms for you to approve."

Heid sighed, pushed to her feet, and accepted the tablet. She stared down at it for a moment and then looked at the tech standing before her. "I need you to help me with something, something just between the two of us. Can you do that?"

"Of course," the woman replied.

Heid pulled out a gray tablet from her cargo pocket and held it out. "I've lost my access on this."

Sylvian frowned as she looked at it. "This isn't CUF technology."

"No, it's not. It will take a bit more finesse to break, I believe. Can you break through its protocols without losing the files?"

"You need it hacked."

"Yes. Can you work on it?"

The tech sighed. "That's not my expertise, but I know the hacker who helped broadcast news of the fungicide last year. She's known to be one of the best out there."

Heid nodded. "Thank you. Be very careful. This tablet can bring trouble to our door if we're not careful."

Sylvian swallowed before nodding. "Understood, captain."

Heid imprinted her approvals on the other tablet and handed it back, and Sylvian moved on. When Heid stepped back into the hallway, she saw more people headed her way. How she wished Sebin were here. He could've organized Tulan Base without breaking a sweat.

As soon as she thought of him, she chided herself. She couldn't think of him. After all, she was the one who'd killed him.

CHAPTER 5

THE DEVIL'S DUE

"SPATE HASN'T CHANGED one bit. It's still a hellhole," Sixx said as he looked out the window of the taxi he and Reyne rode in.

"You grew up here."

"Yeah, so I know firsthand how much of a hellhole it is. The highest crime rate in the Collective, and the highest number of prostitutes per capita in the Collective."

At that moment, they drove by a string of brothels. Prostitutes stood outside, wearing skimpy dresses or tight shorts, depending on their gender. The masks they wore were painted in bright colors.

"That doesn't surprise me in the least," Reyne said.

Spate was a lifeless brown rock except for the community gardens protected by massive glass panes; the lush food orchards paralleled the beauty of gardens found on Myr or Alluvia. The only other thing it had going for it was the perfect combination of human-friendly gravity and atmospheric pressure so that only masks had to be worn to make up for air completely devoid of oxygen and carbon dioxide.

"This whole place still has that same stale smell. You know the stink that old gravity boots have, like sweaty socks left in a locker for a few weeks too long? *That* smell."

Reyne pointed to the rat-like rodents that scoured the surface. "I always attributed it to the vigs. Have you ever gotten a whiff of one of those things up close?"

"Too many times. I learned the hard way that when you're just a scrawny kid and you decide to chase one of them for fun, the whole herd just may decide to chase you back. And those furry little bastards can move fast." Sixx cringed. "I don't know how some people eat those things. They are the devil's spawn."

"Desperation is my guess."

They passed by a caravan of wombies pulling wagons filled with supplies from the docks. The small bumps on their stomachs always made Reyne recoil, but he had to respect how each planet changed the humans who dared to colonize it...sometimes in as little as a couple hundred years.

Wombies, mutated from generations of Spatens who'd survived chiefly on blue tea, had developed an almost camel-like ability to store what little water they took in on the dry world. They were living, shambling reminders that while blue tea could help humans survive on much less water, there were repercussions for playing with human nature. He'd made eye contact with a wombie once, and he could've sworn there'd been no intelligence, let alone humanity, left in those eyes. He looked away from the caravan and checked the time.

"Why did Lincoln have to move the stationhouse so far from the docks?" Reyne muttered. "The old one worked just fine. We're burning over an hour each way that we shouldn't have to."

Sixx chuckled. "Because he wants to take as much money as possible from anyone who lands at Devil Town. All those brothels we passed back there? Notice how the taxi automatically slowed by them? It's not a coincidence so many of Devil Town's diverse services are located on the main road between the docks and the stationhouse."

"At last we're here. Finally," Reyne said.

The taxi followed a line of taxis into a huge circular drive. The stationhouse was a mountain, built out of local brown stone and taller than anything else in Devil Town except for the space docks. Any and all interplanetary business and trading took place at the stationhouse.

When they reached the front entrance, the taxi relayed instructions. *"You have arrived at your destination, the Devil Town stationhouse. The transport charge is thirty-one credits. Please hold your wrist comm under the scanner for payment."*

Reyne frowned as held out his left forearm, which had his comm strapped on it, below the taxi's flashing scanner. "Thirty-one credits? That's robbery."

"You could have three girls for that and still have a credit left over," Sixx said before adding, "Just a guess."

The taxi doors unlocked. *"Thank you for your payment, Mr. Smyth,"* it said, calling Reyne by his cover name. *"Remember to don your breather masks, and have a nice day."*

The two men slid their masks over their faces and emerged from the hovercraft. They had just stepped out before the taxi's next fare rushed past them and hopped in. As with all station-houses, the structure was packed with people during business hours. Reyne didn't miss the CUF drones hovering over the crowd at intervals of thirty feet, give or take. He suddenly found himself thankful for the need to wear breather masks that hid their faces.

The two men moved with the crowd toward the large entrance. Advertisements played on the walls and ceilings as they made slow headway with the herd through the tunnel. Many ads were for blue tea, but there were also ads for prostitutes, sweet soy, and the ever-popular adventure tours through Spate's deserts and canyons.

Other than brands and logos, no advertisements showed words of any kind. Like all fringe colonies, education was a luxury when it was a constant effort to find enough food and water. Generally, only the small minority of colonists who served in the CUF—like Reyne—had learned to read. It was a skill he'd taught to his entire crew.

When they approached the end of the tunnel, the screens transitioned from advertisements to a clip of a beautiful woman removing her mask and inhaling sensually.

Reyne delayed, wishing they could afford cloned skin disguises to hide their identities. Tense, he pulled off his mask and tucked it into his belt. "Be careful not to look up at any screens. They log either one of our faces, we're done for."

"Here goes nothing," Sixx said quietly before sliding off his mask.

They stepped from the tunnel and into a wide-open hall filled with vendors. The smell of food and incense overloaded Reyne's senses, heightened by too many years in space, and he breathed through his mouth. No longer shoulder to shoulder with other traders and customers, the pair strode forward to stand in line before a row of scanners that were mounted across the floor like a series of fence posts. Fortunately, the lines moved quickly as people made appointments with particular traders or vendors, or purchased reservations to the higher-end restaurants or brothels.

When a scanner opened up, Reyne pulled out the pass-card Critch had given him and swiped it over the scanner. The scanner flashed, and a thin computer stick dropped into the tray. Reyne grabbed the stick.

"Welcome to the Devil Town stationhouse, Mr. Smyth, where you're guaranteed to leave satisfied," the stick's sexy, automated

voice said. *"Proceed to the door indicated on the map to begin your adventure."*

A map hologram displayed from the stick. Reyne shot Sixx a quick glance before they moved in unison, weaving around the crowd, careful to give any dromadiers patrolling the area a wide berth.

When they reached a door, the stick spoke again. *"I am your key, Mr. Smyth. Please insert me into the lock. It may be tight, but I'm sure you can make it fit."*

Reyne did as instructed. When he slid the stick into the small opening, the stick emitted a moan of ecstasy.

"Oh, yes. That hits the spot. Thank you, Mr. Smyth. You may now proceed. May your visit to Devil Town fulfill all your fantasies."

The door opened, and the two men stepped through. Whereas the great hall behind them was a bustle of activity, they now found themselves in an empty, winding corridor. Their boot steps echoed as they walked. When a third pair of boot steps joined the echoes, Reyne tensed and noticed Sixx placed his hand over his holster.

The hallway curved, and they then saw the man who was walking toward them. He was tall and well built, similar in size to Sixx, and had the look of a guard about him.

The man sized them quickly up and down. "Follow me." He turned on his heel without waiting for a response.

"I think I liked our last guide better," Sixx said quietly. "I found her to be much more pleasant."

They followed the man down the hallway and into a good-sized lobby, likely used for lavish parties—if the crystal chandeliers, polished floor, and abundance of cushioned loungers and sofas were any indication. Three beautiful women, all skimpily dressed, stopped chatting with one another when the men arrived. Each woman threw a practiced glance at Reyne and Sixx, though their gazes lingered enticingly on Sixx.

"Lincoln will see you now." The guard swiped a pass-card over a scanner on the wall, and a door opened. He motioned for the pair to enter, which they did, and Reyne heard him step inside to stand behind them and alongside two other guards who were already in the office.

If the outer room was lavish, this office was pure opulence. Myrad silver decorated the room from floor to ceiling. Even the gargantuan desk that sat as a centerpiece in the office had silver inlays.

Reyne's gaze fell on the man sitting at the desk. "I see being a stationmaster suits you. I saw a few lovely ladies from your own personal brothel out there."

"I prefer to call it my harem. I like the ring of that better. They service me and my staff in exchange for the safest work environment around, and the most comfortable living in all of Spate's colonies." The paunchy man smiled. "However, I suppose you'd prefer to talk about the other services I provide, Mr. Smyth. Or, may I call you Captain Reyne now?"

Reyne gave a small nod. "It's been a long time, Lincoln."

"Too long. You've put on a few years. Your hair wasn't so gray the last time I saw you."

"And you still had hair the last time I saw you," Reyne responded.

Lincoln shot Reyne a sideways glance before he stood and walked over to Sixx. Several inches shorter than Reyne's man, Lincoln had to look up to meet Sixx's gaze. "You must be the infamous Jeyde Sixx."

"The one and only," Sixx replied.

"Curious. I heard rumors of a couple of my girls not charging you for services rendered. Seems they enjoyed your company a bit too much to consider it work."

Sixx smirked instead of responding.

"Hm. At first, I thought your pretentious Asian features were why I didn't like you. Now I know. You're too cocky for my liking. I'll make sure they charge you double going forward."

Sixx bristled.

Lincoln returned to his desk. "However, since I know you've both been busy, as a courtesy I'll give you each a complimentary service with one of my harem girls today. No charge."

"That's mighty generous of you," Reyne said. "But we came here to discuss business."

"That *is* business." He motioned to two open chairs. "Have a seat."

Reyne took a seat, but Sixx continued to stand behind him.

Lincoln began, "I knew you'd be showing up, or at least one of the other two captains, anyway. Your torrent triad has become quite the news lately. Let me guess—Critch is on Terra talking with Seda Faulk in Rebus Station as we speak."

Reyne narrowed his gaze.

Lincoln shrugged. "Terra is Critch's home world after all. The way I see it, for your revolution to work, you need access to the fringe stations or else you'll run out of food, supplies, and—most importantly—volunteers. With Rebus Station and Devil Town the only two viable fringe stations right now, a wombie could've figured out you'd be showing up at my door. However, I must admit I'm a bit disappointed. No offense, but I was hoping that commandant-turned-torrent would come here to meet with me instead of you."

"You mean Captain Heid," Reyne said.

Lincoln smiled. "Yes, Captain Gabriela Heid. Now she looks like she'd be a fun challenge. Where's she?"

"I don't know. Perhaps she's at Sol Base right now."

Lincoln belted out a laugh. "Good try. We both know Sol Base is out of the picture. Ausyar has half his armada guarding the Collective's little treasure trove. Never mind that it's currently full of rotting corpses, but I'm sure the CUF will just bring in some conscripts to clean up the place once the quarantine from that nasty blight is over. From what I hear, the quarantine coincidentally ends just in time for the cavote harvest."

"How convenient," Reyne muttered. "Just in time for the Collective to get their annual cavote supply."

"I thought so, too." Lincoln leaned back in his chair. "You know, they're still selling the story that you torrents dropped the blight on Sol Base."

Reyne leaned forward. "And what do you think?"

Lincoln guffawed. "Any colonist knows the torrents wouldn't do anything to take down their own fringe stations. They need them too much. It's obvious the Alluvians and Myrads think we're idiots with the stories they feed us through the news. Any colonist with half a brain knows the CUF was behind the blight. They cleared out thousands of colonists who'd been raising quite a stink protesting against Collective control. At the same time, they gained absolute control over the planet's only fringe station, which in turn gained them absolute control over the planet's philoseed and cavote crops."

"Their stationmaster was known to be a bit more fringe-friendly than you," Reyne said. "I heard that you just upped the blue tea provided freely to the CUF by eight percent last month."

Lincoln eyed him. "Where did you hear such a thing?"

"It seems that one of your girls talks in her sleep," Reyne replied.

Lincoln eyed Sixx for a moment before he continued. "It's all business. I was worried that Devil Town was going to be the next fringe station hit with the blight, since Ausyar seemed intent on clearing out the fringe. So I suppose I should thank you for dropping the fungicide on Sol Base, even though the Collective took credit for that. Funny how they blame you for what *they* do and take credit for what *you* do. They've never quite understood how much easier things would be for everyone if they just played it straight from the beginning."

Reyne lifted his chin. "It doesn't matter. The Darions in the other colonies outside Sol Base know the truth. They'll never trade willingly with the Collective again."

"I'm sure they do, but it won't do you any good. I bet you've been trying to reach them, but all you get is radio silence. Am I right?"

He didn't answer.

Lincoln brushed him off. "Don't worry. I'm not digging for information. I know it's true, because I've been trying to reach them, too. The CUF has drones in orbit blocking all communications. I believe Ausyar is making sure that if they don't trade with the Collective, their crops will rot in the fields."

"Why are you trying to contact the Darions? You don't need to negotiate. Your gardens feed everyone here."

"That's the problem. The gardens only feed everyone *here.* Our population is always limited on Spate by the sizes of our gardens. The more food we can import, the more and larger colonies we can build."

"And the richer you become."

Lincoln smiled. "Diversification is always a smart move. A man could always use more credits, especially when they can be used to build space docks."

Reyne frowned. "Why would you build more docks? You already have Devil Town, the largest fringe station in the Collective."

"Redundancies, captain." He paused. "Aren't you from Ice Port?"

His jaw tightened. "I am." *I was.*

"Then you of all people understand the value of redundancies firsthand. When the CUF bombed Ice Port, what happened to Playa's entire support infrastructure? That's right; it collapsed. Unlike here, where we can build protected gardens, Playa's climate is too miserable to support anything. Without any way to import or export, I imagine all of Playa's other colonies have gone extinct by now from starvation. There can't be more than a few thousand Playans left. As a Playan yourself, that makes you a bit of a rarity, doesn't it?"

Reyne glared.

Lincoln smiled, seemingly pleased. "Enough about the other fringe stations. After all, you're here to talk about my fringe station and what it can do for your revolution."

Reyne took a deep breath to calm himself. "As stationmaster, you can control everyone and everything that goes in and out of Spate. That could make you a very powerful ally."

"Or a powerful enemy," Sixx added.

Reyne shot Sixx a hard look before turning back to Lincoln. "The fringe needs your help. The Spatens are as sick of Collective oversight as are all colonists. We deserve equality instead of being treated like second-class citizens. Let us recruit from Spate. In return, we can offer you supplies, rilon, you name it."

"I have a lot to offer a fringe rebellion," Lincoln began. "But that means I also have a lot to lose if I choose the wrong side. Whoever supports torrents will bring Ausyar's armada to their doorstep. As long as I'm neutral, I'm safe and Spate is safe."

"As long as you stay neutral, you've already chosen a side," Reyne refuted.

Lincoln sighed. "My heart beats for the fringe, but my head reminds me that the Collective has been good for business. If I help you, those in power won't take kindly to a stationmaster supporting the fringe." He paused. "They're not calling you torrents. They're calling you terrorists. I don't think it's good for my health or my business to associate with terrorists."

"We may have gotten hold of the fungicide, but Ausyar still

has his hands on the blight. What's to stop him from dropping the blight on Devil Town next? Or, remember what it was like before the Uprising, when colonists weren't allowed to be stationmasters? You think they can't oust you if their mood changes?"

"I know they can," Lincoln snapped back. "Which is exactly why I have to play it safe."

"Be careful about which side you choose," Reyne said. "It just may be the losing side."

Lincoln chortled. "The torrents lost the Uprising. You had the full support of the fringe then. You have a far smaller chance of winning this time."

Reyne remembered every minute detail about the Uprising. He'd spent years working with his counterparts to recruit and build the infrastructure to stand against Alluvia and Myr. And he'd spent years battling alongside those same people—watching many of them die—as they fought for a seat in Parliament. After they lost the Uprising, he'd realized he'd made a mistake. They needed far more than a seat in Parliament to be treated equally. They needed to tear apart the Collective. In his heart, he knew... they would win this time around.

He leaned back. "You're wrong."

"Oh, how so?"

"Because Myr and Alluvia are on the verge of war with each other."

"Rumors," Lincoln said. "I've heard those stories time and time again, yet the two worlds never sway in their mutual control of the Collective."

"If those rumors happen to be true," Reyne said, "what do you think is going to happen to Devil Town when it's caught between the two great powers?"

"It'll be squashed," Sixx interjected. He pinched his fingers together. "Not pretty."

"Pick the right side, Lincoln." Reyne stood. "Give it some thought. We'll be back for your answer."

"Send Gabriela Heid next time. You're a lousy negotiator."

"I'll see what can be arranged, but I should warn you. She's not as nice as I am. I hope you have something far better to offer her than your harem."

Lincoln clapped his hands together. "Oh, I will. I look forward to making her acquaintance. As for today, since you've declined my first offer, I'll offer you information. One piece for each of you."

Reyne's lips thinned. "What's the cost?"

"Who really dropped the blight on Sol Base?" Lincoln asked.

"Ausyar. Everyone knows that."

"I see. Then, I suppose I don't have information for you after all."

The men stared each other down for a lengthy pause.

Reyne broke the silence first. "It's only a rumor, but I heard mention of a secret organization being back in the game."

"The Founders?" Lincoln asked.

Reyne chuckled. "We all know they disappeared centuries ago. Those rumors are obviously farfetched."

Lincoln thought for a moment and then nodded. "Fair enough. Here's my piece of information for you. The CUF is going to crack down on the Space Coast next week."

Reyne rolled his eyes. "That's not information. They've had a quarantine on the Coast for over a year now."

Lincoln shook his head. "You see, Michel Ausyar would never admit it, but he has a weakness for Spaten women. I offer him my personal girls for discretion, even though he tends to be a bit overzealous with them. Anyway, he was bragging how he was going to bomb the hell out of the Space Coast and not break any laws, since it's not officially a part of the Collective. Essentially, they're going to use the asteroids for training practice."

Reyne shrugged. "They'll never reach Nova Colony. It's in the middle of the asteroid belt."

"Perhaps not, but the debris will make it next to impossible for any transports to make it through to Nova Colony." Lincoln sighed. "Maybe you can get word to Nova Colony soon so they can evacuate. No one wants to see colonists starve to death."

He gave a tight nod. "I will. Thank you."

Lincoln then turned to Sixx. "Now, I have a more personal tidbit for you. I've learned that someone you know is a tenured on Myr."

"I know lots of people," Sixx replied with nonchalance. "Be more specific."

Lincoln's lips curled upward. "I believe her name is Qelle."

Reyne's jaw slackened, and he spun to watch Sixx, whose face had drained of all color. His friend leaned on the chair for support. "You're lying."

Reyne turned to Lincoln. "Qelle's dead. It can't be her."

Lincoln shrugged as he leaned back in his plush chair. "What do I have to gain from lying? I'm just sharing what I've learned, because I thought you'd want to know. One of my new girls escaped from a Myrad hauler and ended up at my stationhouse. Long story short, your name is well known around here, and—as you know—girls talk. My new girl recognized your name and thought to share what she knew with me. Anyway, it's a piece of information. Use it as you like."

"Where is she? Who is the girl? Where's the girl now?" Sixx shot the questions at Lincoln.

Lincoln lifted his hand. "That, I can't say."

"Can't or won't?" Sixx asked, his voice getting deeper and harder.

"Can't at this time," Lincoln replied before lifting a finger. "Maintaining her privacy is for her protection. However, I'll see what more information I can dig up, for the right price, of course."

Sixx lunged around the chair and onto the desk. Reyne caught him just before he tackled the stationmaster. The sounds of guns being drawn behind them made Reyne's jaw tighten.

He yanked Sixx back. "You'll get yourself killed," he whispered to his friend.

Lincoln, now red-faced from anger, pushed back from his desk and smoothed his shirt. "We've covered all we're going to cover today. You better be on your way before I have your man arrested."

As the guards escorted Reyne and Sixx to the door, Lincoln added, "Tell Heid I look forward to making her acquaintance."

Reyne's fists remained clenched as they strode out of there and back down the winding hallway. As they walked, he noticed Sixx stared straight ahead.

"She's alive," Sixx said after a lengthy silence, his words carried on an exhale.

"Your wife's dead," Reyne said as gently as possible.

Sixx stopped and faced him. He bore the same dark look he'd borne the day the two men had met. "No, she's not."

CHAPTER 6

ADVENTURES GONE AWRY

WHEN REYNE and Sixx reached the *Gryphon*'s ramp, Sixx froze.

Reyne motioned to the ship. "Come on. The faster we get off this rock, the safer we'll be."

"I'm not going."

"What?"

"I've got to find that girl who knows about Qelle."

Reyne pursed his lips. "I don't know the game Lincoln is playing, but you can't believe anything he says. I can guarantee that he'll make sure you won't get any additional information, not without his chubby hands in the way."

Sixx snarled. "In my gut, I've always known Qelle was alive. Now, to think she's been a slave on Myr all this time?"

"You don't know that."

"It's the only lead I've got. I have to follow it. I'm sorry, boss." He turned to walk away.

"No, Jeyde. I'm sorry," Reyne said. He grabbed Sixx by the shoulder and swung. His fist connected solidly with Sixx's cheek, and the man collapsed. He'd never seen the blow coming. Reyne dragged him up the *Gryphon*'s ramp, to his quarters, and dropped him on his bed.

Reyne entered his captain override code to lock Sixx in his quarters, and headed to the bridge. He strapped in without looking at Throttle. "Get us out of here."

"Hey, Throttle. It's great to see you. I knew you'd be worried since we were gone a few hours and patrols kept cruising by," she rattled off in a low-pitched voice.

"I'll fill you in after we launch," Reyne said.

"Fine." She went through her takeoff procedures and launched from Devil Town's space docks.

From the bridge, he could hear the pounding on Sixx's door.

"Are you going to tell me what's going on?" Throttle asked.

"Sixx isn't too happy with me right now," Reyne replied.

"Why?"

"I punched him." Then he went through the series of events that had transpired in Devil Town.

After he finished his story, Throttle leaned back. "Poor Sixx. Do you trust Lincoln?"

Reyne looked up from the scans he'd been running. "Never. A man doesn't become stationmaster of the largest fringe station without playing both sides. Even so, I believe he was honest about the information with the Space Coast. There was nothing for him to gain by sharing that information, but it could save lives. That's assuming the colonists out there aren't too hardheaded to evacuate."

"What about Sixx's wife?"

He ran a hand through his gray hair. "I don't know. It doesn't make any sense. Her transport ship reported a cat fail— catastrophic failure—but the ship and crew were never recov- ered. While it's possible she survived and was picked up by a Myrad crew, the odds would be low since nothing was ever reported."

"But it is possible." Throttle blew out a breath. "No wonder he's all torn up inside. I'm worried about him."

"I am, too." Reyne looked down at his bruised knuckles. "I am, too."

"Well, let's see if he's come to his senses." He tapped a command to unlock Sixx's door. Immediately, the pounding stopped, and he heard running down the hallway.

Sixx stormed onto the bridge. His hair was disheveled, and a bruise was forming under his eye. "You son of a bitch. You can't force me to not look for my wife. It's my wife we're talking about!"

"Hate me all you want, but I did it for your own good," Reyne snapped back. "Lincoln was maneuvering you into some kind of position that was clearly for his benefit. You're just too blind to see it right now."

His instrument panel chimed. "What now?" He read the caller ID and frowned. "I'm getting a call from the *Honorless*."

"We're supposed to be in radio silence," Throttle said. "We're only to break it in case of an emergency."

He glanced back at Sixx. "This will have to wait."

Sixx was clearly fuming but chose to bite his tongue, lean against the wall, and cross his arms over his chest rather than to continue their argument. He dramatically motioned to Reyne to take the call.

Reyne connected, and Birk's copper-haired visage appeared on the monitor.

"Hello, captain," Birk said with his usual quiet nonchalance.

"What's going on?" Reyne snapped.

The younger man's brows rose before he replied. *"We've run into a situation on Terra. Since you're the nearest to Terra right now—"*

"Just lay it out there."

"Yes, captain. Critch and Chutt left to go to the stationhouse at

Rebus Station. They haven't returned yet, and they're not answering their comms."

"How long ago was that?"

"Twenty-two hours. Their trackers showed them arriving at the stationhouse, but they went offline right after that."

"Shit." Reyne grimaced. "All right. We're heading your way now. Send me your coordinates. We'll be there in..." He glanced at Throttle.

"A little over eleven hours," she said.

"I heard her. Hi, Throttle. How are you?"

"Hey, Birk," she replied with a smile.

"I have the new shocks for your chair. I'll get them to you when you get here."

"Thanks, Birk. You're the best."

Reyne frowned. "Is that all?"

"I've also notified the specters," he continued. *"The* Winter Wind *and* Nighthawk *are both within three days from here."*

"Tell them to hang back for now," Reyne said. "More ships lingering around a single planet means it'll be harder to avoid detection. For all we know, Ausyar has set up a trap for us down there and is using Critch for bait. Let the specters know that we'll keep them updated."

"Will do," Birk said.

"See you soon," Reyne said.

"Oh, be sure to stay on the dark side of Terra," Birk added. *"There's a CUF warship performing maneuvers on the light side."*

"Understood," Reyne said, and he clicked off his comm.

He spun in his seat to face Throttle.

"Change of plans?" she asked.

"Change of plans," he answered. "It looks like we're not heading back to Playa yet after all."

"I'll need to drop us out of jump speed to change course."

"Do what you need to do."

Throttle broadcast to the engine room. "Hey, Boden. We're dropping from jump speed and then going right back into it. So hold on for the next few minutes. I don't want you to bruise your shin like last time."

"*What's going on?*" came Boden's response.

"We're going to Terra," she replied.

"*Oh. Okay,*" Boden replied.

Reyne turned back to Sixx, who was still glaring at him. He pointed to Sixx's swollen eye. "I'm sorry about that. Lincoln clearly has something planned for you, and I was trying to stop you from walking into that weasel's trap. Now, I give you my word that after we resolve this situation on Terra, finding Qelle will be this crew's highest priority. I will do everything in my power to help you find Qelle. Is that fair enough?"

"Don't forget me," Throttle added. "We're all in this together."

Sixx didn't take his eyes off Reyne. After an unbearable silence, he gritted out, "Fair enough." He took his seat and buckled in. "That doesn't change the fact that you were an asshole back there."

Reyne nodded and pointed to his own cheek. "You can take one free swing at me. Any time, any place. Will that make us equal?"

Sixx's eye twitched. "I don't hit old guys."

The corner of Reyne's lip curled.

"I haven't been back to Terra in a long time," Throttle said.

"Well, it should make for an interesting visit," Reyne said. "It's the one place in the entire Collective that wants me dead more than the CUF wants me dead."

CHAPTER 7

THE TRAITOR OF TERRA RETURNS

THE *GRYPHON* ATTACHED alongside the *Honorless* on the far side of Terra's smaller moon. There, the two crews met to discuss the situation and brainstorm options. However, the topic kept digressing.

"I don't know what else to tell you," Gabe, the pilot of the *Honorless* said with a hint of exasperation. "Not long after they entered the stationhouse to meet with Seda, we lost contact. Either Seda has a dampener to block signals, or they're dead. If it's the former, we would've heard something from them by now. If it's the latter, there's nothing we can do and we should hightail it out of here."

"You're giving up on the captain too easily," Birk chided. "This ship isn't yours to take."

"Oh, yeah?" Gabe replied. "I'm the pilot. If it's not mine, then whose is it?"

"The *Honorless* belongs to Critch until we have tangible proof of his demise."

"Enough," Reyne jumped in, frustrated at the bickering and none too pleased with how close Birk was sitting next to Throttle.

"Let's not start dividing Critch's possessions, shall we? First, I'm going down to the surface to meet with Seda to get to the bottom of this."

"That might be a bad idea," Throttle said. "If Seda killed Critch and Chutt, he could just as easily kill you."

"Thanks for the vote of confidence," Reyne replied drily. "If Seda intends to do me harm, he'll have a harder time since I'm going to make him come to me. Somewhere where we can better control the situation."

"It'll have to be someplace private," Sixx said. "Too many people will recognize you down there, and not in a good way."

Reyne nodded. "I know just the place."

Three hours later, the *Gryphon* landed at Rebus Station. Rather than taking a taxi, Reyne, Sixx, and Birk walked the two kilometers to their destination. He knew Sixx could use the physical activity due to the stress he'd been carrying around. It was late in the day, but the streets bustled with activity.

The colony still bore scars from the battles that had taken place during the Uprising. Empty, bombed-out buildings stood as ghostly reminders of the young men and women who'd died under Reyne's command. A day hadn't gone by when he didn't see their faces in his dreams.

Bone-deep exhaustion ebbed through his stiff joints. It was a fatigue he'd carried with him for two long decades, as though every life lost under his command was another lead weight he had to carry as penance.

When the rendezvous place came into view, Sixx frowned. "That's definitely not what I had in mind when I was talking about someplace private."

Reyne let old memories pour through his mind as he looked

at the sign, which read:

LAST DROP CAFÉ

Critch and he had drunk far too many drinks to count at that bar. It had been their regular haunt during the Uprising, the place they'd go to toast victories won and commiserate lives lost. Unfortunately, there'd been too many of the latter.

From the look of the exterior, the place hadn't changed in the last twenty years, an assumption Reyne was banking on. He nodded to the bar. "It has a basement they use for storage. It should be safe from peering ears and eyes."

"But we still have to walk through the bar where there's going to be just the sort of Terran who may recognize you," Sixx said.

Reyne tugged his hat lower to hide as much of his face as possible. "If there's any place around Rebus Station that offers a level playing field, this is it."

"There are worse places to die than in a bar," Birk murmured.

Reyne and Sixx both stopped and looked at the pirate.

"We're not going to die today," Sixx said.

"You say that because you're an optimist," Birk said. "I'm a realist. And I think we need more guns."

"Come on," Reyne said. "Let's get this over with."

They crossed the street and Sixx strode into the bar first, followed by Reyne, then Birk. About a dozen stony men sat around the bar. Each looked like he came there every day, sat in the same chair every day, and drank out of the same glass every day.

All eyes turned toward them.

"Good afternoon, gentlemen," Sixx said as he strode in with his usual calmness.

Reyne watched the floor, making sure the brim of his hat covered much of his face as he followed his friend to the bar and took a seat. He gave Sixx a quick nod, and the man leaned on the bar and motioned the bartender.

Sixx spoke quietly but clearly. "I hear you have a room downstairs that could be used by customers who prefer to have a more discreet conversation."

The bartender remained stoic. "I don't have any such room."

Sixx slid several credits across the counter.

"Oh, that room. It's already booked full."

Sixx slid across several more credits.

"I don't see why you couldn't use it for the next hour or so."

Sixx handed him another few credits. "I'll take three of your house whiskeys. Make mine a double."

"Coming right up."

As the bartender poured their drinks, Reyne felt like he was being watched. He glanced around to find a craggy old man with wiry hair at the far end of the bar staring intently at him. The man's gray gaze narrowed. "I know you."

Reyne looked away, pretending to ignore him.

"The traitor of Terra has returned!"

Every occupant in the bar turned.

"Well, damn." Sixx pulled out his pistol.

Reyne sighed. "Here we go again."

"Still think we're not dying today?" Birk asked as he took a stance between Reyne and the Terrans as he also unholstered his pistol.

"Well, *I'm* not dying today," Sixx said. "I'm not so sure about our intrepid captain."

Chairs creaked against the wood floors as men pushed off from their chairs and moved in on the trio.

"Now would be a good time to explain that Doc was the traitor," Sixx said.

"You really think they'd believe me?" Reyne asked.

"No."

"No," Birk echoed.

"You've got some nerve coming back here, traitor," the old man said. "I lost a lot of good friends because of you."

Birk tutted and aimed his pistol at the nearest man. "That's close enough."

"Traitor!"

A man spat. Reyne grimaced when he felt the spittle hit his jacket.

"Traitor!" another chanted.

"Kill him!"

"Yeah!"

"Hands off. He's with me," a booming voice called out from the doorway.

The crowd immediately parted for the newcomer.

"That's the traitor of Terra," a man complained.

The newcomer ignored the comment and approached Reyne and his protectors. The man's demeanor and aura exuded as much authority as his voice, and no one else raised an objection.

"You've always had impeccable timing," Reyne said.

Seda glanced around the room before turning back to Reyne. "I see your reputation precedes you."

Reyne glanced over Seda's shoulder. "What, no guards?"

"Oh, they're nearby if I need them. I don't need them, do I?"

"I'm just here to talk." Reyne came to his feet and motioned to the door behind the bar. He took the lead, and Seda followed him. Sixx and Birk remained at the top of the stairs, standing guard.

Reyne took the stone steps down to the small basement, and memories of torrent planning meetings held in that place brought raw emotions to the surface. In the dark, he walked to the center of the room and pulled the string to click on the room's single light. Everything was exactly as he remembered.

"At first I thought it was odd you chose a bar for our meeting," Seda said. "Now your choice makes perfect sense." He looked around. "I suppose this is one of the locations where the torrent marshals met. I've always wondered where around Rebus Station your secret meeting rooms were."

"It's not something we shared with those on the wrong side of the fight, like you."

Seda took a seat on a barrel of whiskey. "I was serving as a conscript at the far end of the Collective during much of the Uprising. As I'm sure you remember, it's not exactly easy for a conscript to escape from a CUF warship's deck in the middle of space."

Reyne grabbed another barrel and sat. "I'm not interested in ancient history. I'm much more interested in things that have happened over the past couple of days."

"You're here for Critch."

"Do you know where he is?"

"Of course. I turned him and his man over to the CUF. He's at the Citadel."

Reyne's blood ran cold. "You're lying. If the CUF had him, his capture would be playing nonstop on all the news channels."

"They don't know they have Critch. Both he and Chutt are there under fake identifications. I assure you that they were processed correctly. The dromadiers who brought Critch and Chutt to the Citadel are on my payroll." He pulled out a tablet and showed a video of two men, both in restraints, being escorted into the Citadel. Their faces looked different—they were likely wearing cloned skin—but the way each man moved was unmistakable.

"How much did they pay you to sell out your own brethren?"

Seda held up a hand. "It's not like that. Not at all." He looked around and grabbed a bottle off the shelf. He dusted it off, popped the cork, and took a drink before he spoke again. "You know they won't even acknowledge that you're trying to restart the Uprising. They're calling it an unrest." He chuckled, though the sound was devoid of humor. "An unrest." He shook his head.

He handed the bottle to Reyne, who drank from it before handing it back. "What's that have to do with turning Critch over to the CUF?"

"Everything." Seda took another drink. "Do you know why they built the Citadel here, not far from Rebus Station?"

"Yes. Because here is where so much of the Uprising took place."

Seda nodded. "The Citadel was built to house torrents, not criminals. It was a prisoner-of-war camp before it they rebranded it as a prison. However, none of the early prisoners were ever released. Political prisoners continue to be brought in, but no one leaves and very few escape."

"And now Critch is stuck in there."

"You don't understand. He *volunteered*."

Reyne guffawed. "That would never happen."

"It would and it did. I made a proposal to him and he accepted. When he learned of a mutual friend who was imprisoned in the Citadel—"

"What's the prisoner's name?"

"Ice Port's stationmaster. Vym Patel. I believe you know her quite well."

Reyne leaned forward. "Vym's alive?"

Seda nodded. "According to my sources, Ausyar took his time interrogating her before sending her to the Citadel to rot. Now you can see why Critch volunteered to go inside the walls."

"And if Ausyar learns that Critch is in there, what do you think he'll do? He'll make Vym's interrogation look like a dinner date."

"That's why I'll make sure we get Critch out of there before anyone suspects his real identity."

Reyne's gaze narrowed. "Vym and Critch are friends, but I'm

not buying it. You're telling me Critch just up and volunteered to help break Vym out of there?"

"No," Seda said with a partial smile. "He volunteered to help me break *everyone* out. We're taking the Citadel down once and for all."

He belted out a laugh. "You've been drinking too much Terran whiskey if you think taking down the Citadel is possible."

"It's more possible than you may think."

Reyne watched him for a moment as he sobered. "You're serious."

"I'm deadly serious. There are over twenty thousand Terrans imprisoned within the Citadel, with only walls and drones keeping them in there."

"You make it sound simple."

"I wish it were. Researching the Citadel has been a pet project of mine for years. Breaking into the Citadel is easy. If I knew the location of Vym's cell, I could have her free by morning. The challenge lies in trying to free *all* the prisoners. Cutting a hole into every cell isn't practical, as the CUF would send in reinforcements by the time we cleared only five or ten cells. I need a way to open up the entire Citadel without risking the lives of the people inside, and have them all safely out of there before the CUF is any the wiser."

Reyne stared at the other man as he considered Seda's words. Was it possible? Could they take down the Citadel? Reyne had long fantasized about freeing all those inside, but his thoughts on it had always been just that—a fantasy.

"Have you thought about taking control of the Citadel?" Reyne asked finally.

"Yes, but the systems would be difficult to hack. The Citadel is fully automated. The only way to take control of the prison is to turn off the power. The problem with doing that is it's a self-enclosed system. I can't hit it with an EMP because the Citadel is essentially a giant Faraday cage, which protects all its systems from any form of outside electronic attack. Trust me, I've tried. Even if I set off an EMP inside the prison, I'd fry the systems, but the Citadel's backup generators would restore power within seconds. And those generators are within *another* Faraday cage. Essentially, I would need to release two EMPs within seconds of each other—one near the generators and one inside the prison. It's proved to be a challenge I've struggled to overcome."

Reyne frowned. "It doesn't sound so complicated if you use a two-pronged attack. One team to fry the generators, one team to set off an EMP inside the walls."

"I wish it were that simple. The Citadel covers five square kilometers. I've come across very basic schematics, but they don't reveal the location of the generators. I've interviewed the only two still-living escapees, and neither could provide information about the generators. I've attempted to acquire inside sources, but the only staff are roughly a dozen desk jockeys to keep the systems running smoothly, and they live within the walls. I ran out of options and needed someone inside with the skills to locate the Citadel's power generators and identify any other potential problems. We both know Critch is the best when it comes to precisely this type of job."

Reyne grabbed the bottle from Seda and took another drink. "Even so, Critch would never have gone in there without a plan to get out of there on his own."

"He has two plans. I embedded two pieces of tech in Critch's forearm under his wrist comm. A tracker so I can come to him, and a micro-EMP that he can use to help open his escape route should there be a problem."

"All comms are removed, so any scan run after they were removed would pick up hardware he was carrying."

"Since they require tools to remove, the most thorough body scans are done at time of arrest, before the comms are removed.

Any cursory follow-up scans aren't as thorough and wouldn't pick up this hardware. It's too high-tech."

"You seem confident."

"It's very expensive hardware."

Reyne sighed as he ran through scenarios in his head, hitting walls on every scenario. Finally, he spoke. "What were the next steps?"

"I wait until I get the signal from Critch...or Chutt, who is wearing the same implants."

"What's the signal?"

"If they press the tracker on their arms, it emits a flashing beacon at their location. It's their signal to let me know to come for them, and I hope that they've acquired the information I need."

Reyne held up a finger. "You need to provide me access to their trackers along with all information you have on the Citadel. I need everything you've got."

He pulled out a computer card. "I already anticipated you'd ask for that."

Reyne pocketed the card. "You sell a good story. But how do I know that you didn't sell this same story to Critch just be able to turn him over to the CUF without him putting up a fight? Those two pirates would be worth several hundred thousand credits, if not more."

"As I told you, the CUF has no idea they have Critch AKA Drake Fender or Chutt AKA Chutney Rios locked in their prison. According to their systems, their latest additions are two drunks who assaulted a citizen in the middle of Rebus Station."

"How did you fool the biometrics scans?"

"That was easy. The harder part was convincing Critch and Chutt."

Reyne watched him for a lengthy pause. "Why are you doing this? You have the best job a colonist can have. You make money by ensuring Terra stays under the heel of the Collective. What's in it for you to go against the Collective?"

Seda shot him a hard look. "I'm taking action because the Collective is broken. When I was younger, I believed the Collective would settle into a sustainable balance across all six worlds, but I no longer believe that is possible. There have been too many things done to ensure power remains on the two citizen worlds."

"Balance, huh?" Reyne eyed Seda while he took a long swig. He wiped his mouth with the back of his hand. "I met a man last year who talked about balance. In fact, he seemed obsessed with the concept." He nodded toward Seda. "You're one of them, aren't you?"

"One of who?"

"The Founders."

Seda's brows rose. "I have no idea what you're talking about."

"Hm." When Reyne handed the bottle back to Seda, he pulled out his pistol and pressed it against the man's chest. Seda, seemingly unbothered by the assault, held out his hands in surrender, and Reyne began patting the man's pockets.

"What are you looking for?" Seda asked, almost sounding bored.

Reyne continued patting him down until he came to a pocket on Seda's calf. He pulled out a gray tablet and held it up for the stationmaster to see before dropping it on his lap.

"Not a Founder, my ass."

Seda reached down and grabbed the tablet. "It's dangerous for you to speak of such things." He then moved in a blur, knocking the gun out of Reyne's hands. The next instant, Reyne found himself on the floor.

Seda stood over Reyne, his lips pursed. After a pause, he reached down to help Reyne to his feet.

Reyne rubbed his now-sore neck. "You could've knocked my gun away at any time. Why did you let me search you?"

"I wanted to see how much you knew. Now I understand why Mason hates you so much. You could make life much harder for the Founders if you so choose. Not that Mason isn't doing a fine job of that on his own." He reclaimed his seat and slid the tablet back into his pocket. "Oh, and you're wrong on one point. Mason talks about balance, but it's power he's obsessed with, not balance."

"They're probably one and the same in his mind," Reyne said.

"I'm curious," Seda began. "Was it Gabriela Heid who shared our secrets? She's the first Founder believed to have betrayed the cause in over a century."

"I thought your cause was about equality across the Collective. As a torrent, that's exactly what she's fighting for."

Seda lifted his chin. "Equality was the goal." He cocked his head. "So it was Gabriela Heid who told you about the Founders."

"No. I tracked her down using another Founder's tablet."

"I find that difficult to believe, as these tablets are coded to each specific Founder's DNA. This individual would've had to code their tablet to you. Who was it?"

"I'll tell you another time." Reyne paused. "So, what name do you go by? Cook? Shoemaker? Candlestick Maker?"

The corners of his lips curled upward. "I'll tell you another time."

Reyne eyed him. "Fair enough." He walked over and picked up the bottle of whiskey that had fallen to the floor and handed it to Seda. "Tell me more about your plan for how to get our army out of the Citadel."

"Our army?"

Reyne gave a nod. "If I'm not mistaken, we have over twenty thousand torrents stuck within those walls who are more than ready for a little payback."

CHAPTER 8

SETTING UP THE CHESSBOARD

"I THINK TAKING down the Citadel has to be our next action," Reyne finished sharing his thoughts on the Terra situation.

"*I don't like it,*" Heid replied, her voice sounding tinny since she was speaking through her wrist comm. "*There are too many variables we can't control.*"

"I don't like it either, but I also don't see an alternative. Seda's lined up the chess pieces. He's waiting to see if we'll play."

"*We can't trust Seda until we know who he really is. Are you sure he didn't drop any hints as to his Founder pseudonym? Besides Vym, there's only one Founder in the fringe I'd consider trusting, and that's Aeronaut. The odds of Seda being him are low.*"

"Just do a search on Seda Faulk in the system. See if you recognize him as one of your Founder buddies."

"*It's not that easy. I've only ever met a couple of Founders from the fringe in person, and they both wore cloned skin. Until we know for sure, we have to assume Mason is pulling the strings of any Founder you meet.*"

"I said we'd play along. I never said I'd blindly follow Seda's plan, let alone trust him. Hell, I'm assuming he's playing us. When he makes his move against us, I am going to make damn well sure we're ready to fire back with moves of our own."

"I can't believe Critch let himself get arrested. He's going to get himself killed pulling stunts like this. I'm going to strangle that infuriating man for not talking it over with us first." She sighed. *"I can have the* Arcadia *prepped and on the way to Terra in under three hours."*

"No way. You know our rule. After the *Matador* mess, we can't risk all three of us in the same place at the same time. Besides, we need you at Tulan Base. If we lose the Base or the *Arcadia*, we lose everything."

"Then send in the specters."

"Not yet. We're even keeping the *Gryphon* and *Honorless* off the surface for now. Bringing in more of the fleet will only raise suspicion and draw Ausyar's attention. If the armada moves in on Terra, we'd be stranded here. Besides, the fleet can't be of much help. This is a ground operation, not a fleet op."

A long silence.

"You still there?"

"...Yes."

"Listen, we don't even know if Critch is still alive."

Another silence.

"The chance that he is—or Vym is—is well worth the risk. Believe me, I understand why you have to go in. I'd go in, too, if I were there. I just don't like how the odds are stacked against us."

"Trust me, I don't like the situation any better than you do. If Critch volunteered, he had a backup plan. Hell, that guy has backup plans for his backup plans. He wouldn't have let himself get arrested unless he was sure he had a way out."

"Except, knowing him, that fool probably thinks he can just walk right out of the Citadel."

Reyne chuckled, picturing exactly the same thing.

"Keep me posted. I'll have the Arcadia *prepped and ready to jump if you need assistance. Oh, and Reyne? Don't you get yourself killed."*

"Take care of yourself, kiddo."

He turned off the comm. His jaw tightened, and then he hit his console. "Damn it."

He closed his eyes, inhaled deeply, and leaned back in his seat. Reyne, Heid, and Critch had formed a leadership triad to ensure the Uprising wouldn't fail if one—or even two—were killed. But that oversimplified the truth.

Reyne and Heid were expendable. Reyne would forever carry the weight of being seen as a traitor, even though the truth was very different. Heid was a citizen, and would never be accepted as a colonist. Critch never thought himself any more important than them, but he was the heart and soul of the torrents. Critch was the only leader who'd never ceased embodying the true torrent spirit.

Critch had served alongside Reyne as a torrent marshal in the first Uprising. He'd then changed his identity to escape the CUF when they searched to arrest or kill all torrent leaders. He became a pirate, spending the next twenty years stealing from the Collective and planning a new rebellion. Every torrent trusted Critch, and would follow him anywhere. If he died—and the torrents were left with a rumored traitor and a citizen as their leaders—the fire that had been building for the new Uprising could all too easily flicker and die.

If there was any chance that Critch was still alive, Reyne *had* to go in. That knowing part, deep in his gut, warned him that trusting Seda could be a deadly mistake. Seda Faulk had become rich off the Collective. The stationmaster was a Founder, giving Reyne another reason to not trust him. Could Reyne keep one move ahead of Seda?

He wasn't so sure, but he didn't have any other option.

CHAPTER 9

FRESH MEAT

"STOP THAT."

"Stop what?"

Critch motioned to Chutt's face. "You're wriggling your nose. It's annoying."

"My face itches."

"If you keep acting all twitchy, you're going to draw attention to us." Critch's face also itched, but he was careful to not scratch at the cloned skin they each wore to disguise their features. He scanned the open prison area where they spent twelve hours each day.

It was a drab, desolate place. Terran stone floors and walls, populated by thousands of prisoners in the same gray garb. They stood, sat, and lay around—often in small groups—and passed the hours with talking, invisible games, or simply waiting until it was time to return to their cells. Some worked out to stay fit. Others were about to pass through to the abyss. Still others wore shifty expressions, as though planning an escape. The Citadel provided the minimal requirements: food, shelter, baths, and clothing. Beyond that, the prisoners were left to their own devices.

Critch maintained a stone face so as not to betray the real reason he and Chutt were in the Citadel. He nodded to one of the food lines. "Let's grab some grub."

Like everything in the Citadel, the food lines were automated. Prisoners got one ration loaf per day. If a prisoner tried to take someone else's ration, the drones shocked him. If a prisoner didn't take a ration, the drones didn't do anything. Within the Citadel's walls, life had no value. If prisoners rioted, drones did nothing. If one gang attacked another gang, the drones did nothing. If a prisoner was caught trying to escape—which seemed to be a daily occurrence—the drones shot him.

As they proceeded to the line, Critch felt gazes upon them from the other prisoners, especially the gangs. The pair hadn't been at the Citadel a week yet, and Critch imagined they were getting sized up for what kinds of problems they might cause, or if they'd make potential allies. Either option made sense. Critch and Chutt were both obviously fit, though Chutt had over fifty pounds of muscle on Critch. Most of the prisoners were scrawny from years of surviving on too few calories and not enough activity.

Critch knew that no one recognized them because of their cloned skin masks. If someone had recognized him, he had no doubt his notoriety would end him up in Ausyar's torture chambers in no time flat. However, Critch recognized plenty of his fellow prisoners. He estimated about half of the prisoners had served in the Uprising, with the other half being political dissidents, those who got in the way of the wrong person, and even a few criminals.

Critch had seen dozens of faces that brought back memories of the Uprising. The gaunt prisoners were nearly unrecognizable after twenty years in prison. Even so, Critch had no problem spotting the torrents who'd served under him. And it damn near crushed his soul seeing those brave souls in that hellhole.

They grabbed their rations and sat down at a small table. A man and a woman sat eating their rations at a nearby table. Critch didn't recognize her, but seeing the man was a punch to the gut. Luther had been only sixteen years old when he signed on as a torrent in the Uprising. The young boy had been full of energy and passion, though Critch was only five years older than him. Critch had seen him perform admirably in several battles, and had always hoped Luther was one of the lucky ones who escaped the CUF.

He wasn't.

Luther was thirty-seven now, though he could easily pass for fifty-seven. He held the woman's hand while they each chewed on their ration loaf. The rations obviously contained more than just a hash of cavote and philoseed because, with all the sex and rapes that happened around the prison area, Critch had yet to see a pregnant woman, let alone a baby.

Critch made eye contact with Luther. The man's gaze narrowed briefly before he shook off whatever thought he'd had and returned his attention to the woman.

"I've been keeping an eye out," Chutt began, his rough-voiced whisper sounding like sandpaper. "And, the drones stay off our backs. It wouldn't be too hard for someone who really knows demolitions to make some serious product here."

"Someone just like you, I'd wager," Critch said softly before taking a bite out of the oily, chewy loaf that tasted a little of nuts and a lot of nothing.

Chutt hefted his ration. "Take this brick, for instance. It's got enough philoseed in it that if you rolled out a decent length and dried it out, you'd have a flexible wick. Steam the soap and you have yourself highly combustible gas. I've seen plenty of usable containers around here that are being used for moonshine."

Critch considered for a moment. "You could build a bomb for the generator."

"Of course. And building an EMP for the overall prison will be even easier. All I need is at least four of those humidifying coils in the showers to extend the range of this little baby." He held up his forearm where the micro-EMP had been implanted.

"That won't be easy. Then again, things never are. So, you'd work on Plan D while I scout the generator situation?" Chutt's personal favorite plan was Plan D, which stood for Plan Destroy. Critch liked having more than one plan. The more options available meant the better their chance at succeeding.

Chutt's lip curled upward. "I tell you, it'll work. I've had plenty of time to work out the details in my head. We could have everything set to blow and then call Seda for pickup. If things hit the shitter, we just call Seda for pickup and then go through with his fancy plan."

"It could work." Critch thought about his friend's idea. If they took down the Citadel from the inside, the CUF would be none the wiser that he or Seda were involved. Seda's plan, on the other hand, guaranteed the CUF would know the prisoners had outside help and would send in plenty of heat, making it a challenge to leave Terra quietly.

Chutt shrugged. "Hell, we've been in here six days, and I'm already dying from boredom. I can't even pass the time with sex because I can tell you I haven't been here near long enough for any of the women around here to look attractive."

"How soon can you make it happen? Whatever we do, we need to get it done and get out of here fast. I don't think we can keep avoiding the gangs trying to recruit us, and I get the feeling they don't take rejection well."

"I could have the bomb built tomorrow and the EMP the next day, assuming you create a diversion when I go for the coils."

"A diversion I can handle."

"So what do you think?"

Critch glanced over at Luther before turning back to Chutt.

He tore off a portion of his loaf, made sure he wasn't in the line of any drone's sight, and slid it over to Chutt. "Let's do it."

Chutt grinned and grabbed the extra food and smashed it into his loaf. He stood. "I think I'll go get myself some supplies so I can start making my toys tonight."

Critch stood. "Meet here fifteen before shift change to debrief. I need to scout out the generators. If you don't need my EMP, I'll put it to use."

Chutt waved him off. "Have fun with it."

The men separated. Chutt headed off to the showers while Critch headed to the alley that led to a door that no prisoner was allowed to go through—alive, anyway. It was the "back door," the one where all deceased prisoners were brought for incineration. It was also the only door Critch knew wasn't locked.

Critch approached slowly. He knew from running tests yesterday that if he walked slow and meandered his way toward the door, he could touch it before waking a drone and getting shocked. But the shock hurt like hell.

He paused every few seconds to make sure he wasn't being watched and that no drones had woken. With five meters to go, he moved even slower, taking small bites out of his loaf. When he was less than a meter away, he leaned against the wall near the door. Pretending to be lost in thought, he closed his eyes and focused on listening to the constant humming of the drones in the open area. He could hear many layers of hums, some closer, others distant. Only one hum remained constantly near, roughly ten meters at his two o'clock high.

He was being watched.

Drones were easier to handle than human guards. Drones were purely rational and reliable. They would react the same way to the same situation every single time. It made Critch's job easier.

He reached out for the door and heard the drone zoom in.

According to Seda, the micro-EMP in his arm was weak enough that it wouldn't raise alarms. If a single drone dropped, the Citadel's human techs would assume the drone had broken down. They'd come to repair it rather than call in backup.

In a rush, he grabbed the lever and slid the door open just as the drone fired a shocker blast. The door stopped the blast, and Critch squeezed his arm. Critch waited for the shock, but instead heard a thump as the drone fell to the ground. His micro-EMP had worked, though it was good for only one shot. He scanned the area for more drones coming at him, but the fallen drone hadn't alerted others. Critch stepped out from behind the door, saw the dead drone, and kicked it through the door and into the darker hallway beyond.

He was about to step inside when he froze. At a table in the distance, an old, frail woman watched him intently. She hadn't been frail the last time he'd seen her, only a year ago. But, her eyes were as sharp as ever.

Vym.

Critch took a step toward her, but stopped himself and pulled the door closed, cutting him off from Vym and the open prison area. She was alive—that was all he needed to know. If he didn't find the generator, he had no chance of getting her out of there. He had to focus, even though every bone in his body was shouting at him to go talk to her, to reveal his identity so she knew she'd soon be safe.

Instead, he bent down and examined the spherical drone. It had no eye mechanism, only a body heat scanner. On its back was a triangle-shaped patch, the same patch on the vests worn by the Citadel's human staff. He peeled off the beacon and stuck it onto the front of his shirt. Then, he took off at a run.

He ran as quickly as he could down the hallway while still taking in anything that hinted that a generator may be near, such as cables or signs. Small drones perched near the ceilings but none woke, thanks to the gamble he'd made that the patch he wore was an all-safe signal. He ran past the incinerator and continued. He didn't have much time before a tech would come for the drone, so he pushed himself, even after his breathing became ragged.

Just as he began to doubt the direction he'd chosen, he came across the generator. A massive engine sitting within a large cage —a Faraday cage. He frowned as he memorized all its features. While the generator was large, it wasn't big enough to power the entire Citadel. He scoured the room, but saw nothing.

With a curse, he spun on his heel and sprinted back to the dead drone. By the time he reached it, he could hear talking down the other hallway. He tore off the patch and stuck it back onto the drone, careful to place it in the same location as it had been before. He pressed open the door and kicked the drone back outside. He'd not long shut the door when another drone shocked him.

Agony tore through Critch and he fell to the ground in a spasm. By the time he recovered his senses, the dead drone was gone, taken by the techs. He was still alive, which meant they'd suspected nothing. Idiots.

He pushed himself to his feet and saw that Vym was nowhere to be found. No one seemed to be watching him, though he had no doubt he'd been seen by many. He stumbled his first few steps until he found his bearings, and then walked toward his and Chutt's table. Critch was a bit early, but Chutt was often early. There was no sign of him.

Critch looked across the wide open area, looking for Chutt's larger, taller figure in a sea of gray. Finding nothing, he began to walk around, careful to ignore any gang members he came across. When he heard a yell, he veered toward the direction of the noise. He didn't have to go far. The activity was near the gang that provided all the population's moonshine.

Mingh had been a torrent who served under Critch during the Uprising. Critch had never liked the guy. He'd had a mean streak then, and seemed to have become meaner from his years spent in the Citadel. Critch had caught his gaze once, and had seen the truth. Mingh missed war. He'd been looking for it ever since.

Right now, Mingh was focusing his rage at a prisoner his gang has grabbed. Critch approached with trepidation, already suspecting what had happened. His gut instinct didn't fail him. Sure enough, Chutt was lying on the ground, bloodied from taking a solid beating.

Critch took a step forward, but someone pulled him back. "Don't do it. They'll just do the same to you."

He turned to find Luther. The man didn't show any sign of recognizing Critch.

"The Minks caught him trying to steal," Luther continued. "It's already too late for him. Look."

Critch looked back to his friend to find him panting hard, harder than Critch had ever seen him breath. He then noticed the bloodied puncture marks in Chutt's shirt, nearly hidden by all the blood from Chutt's beating.

Critch's jaw and fists clenched as he watched his friend drown in his own blood. It took nearly ten minutes before Chutt suffocated, and Critch never took his eyes off him. Once Chutt's body relaxed completely, the prisoners dispersed. Critch didn't leave. He stood there until there was only one other person remaining, watching him. *Mingh.*

Critch wanted to slam into the bastard and tear out his throat. He could easily kill him before Mingh's gang killed Critch. But if Critch died, all hope of freeing the prisoners died with him.

Mingh bore a cruel sneer on his face while he continued to watch Critch. Forcing himself to turn away first went against every fiber of Critch's being, but he did. Mingh laughed, and finally walked away.

Mingh believed Critch feared him. He couldn't have been more wrong.

With everyone gone, Critch knelt beside his friend's body. Chutt's expertise in demolitions surpassed anyone in the Collective. *Such a waste.*

He pulled out the small arrowhead he'd carved his first night at the Citadel. Critch had grown up on Terra and—like most Terrans—he knew how to work the onyx-hard stone into useful tools as well as deadly weapons. He grabbed Chutt's forearm and made a single, long slice. He dug into his friend's warm blood until he found the micro-EMP. He stood and said a final prayer over Chutt's body.

A siren blasted throughout the Citadel, signaling shift change. As Critch walked back to his cell, he began to devise new plans. But his thoughts kept fading back to memories of a lost friend.

CHAPTER 10

STICKY SITUATIONS

"CHUTT'S TRACKER HAS GONE OFFLINE," Reyne said as he walked into Seda's office at Rebus Station. "What's that mean?"

Seda looked up from his screen. "The trackers go offline if they can't read vitals. It means Chutt's either dead, they cut the tracker out of him, or he hit his EMP."

"Could the signal be blocked?"

Seda shook his head. "These are interplanetary trackers we're talking about. With Chutt on Terra, there should be nothing capable of blocking his signal."

Reyne considered their options. "We have to initiate the plan."

Seda leaned back. "We can't go in after Critch until he's found the generators. If we go in for him too soon, we could blow our chance at freeing everyone. Besides, if the prison's scans catch you or any of your crew on the screens, Ausyar will know there are torrents on Terra. We have to play it safe."

"No," Reyne said with finality. He paused and took a seat.

"Listen, their cover is likely already blown. If Chutt is offline, how much time do you think Critch has?"

"You have to give it time. Critch hasn't hit his tracker yet. Be patient."

"I *am* the patient one. If I were in there, Critch would've broken me out two days ago. I'm going in with or without your help."

"These things have to be planned carefully. You've seen the schematics for yourself. You can't just go in half-cocked. Listen, I've analyzed every escape from the Citadel. There have been six successful escapes and forty-seven near-successful escapes in the past twenty years."

"What constitutes a near-successful escape?" Reyne asked.

"A near-successful escape is when they make it outside the Citadel, only to be killed within the first three days. You know why so many are unsuccessful?"

Reyne waited for an answer.

"Because the CUF has more dromadiers patrolling Rebus Station than any other fringe station."

"I noticed that. I had a hell of a time getting to your office without being caught."

"You didn't need to come here. I could've met you at the Last Drop Café again."

"We don't have time for scheduling meetings. We have to get to the Citadel."

"You realize that even if you get Critch out of there, as soon as the alarms sound you'll have hundreds of dromadiers called in. Based on the past escape attempts, they'll arrive on site in as few as twelve minutes."

"Twelve minutes? I can work with that."

"I need a drink." Seda stood and walked over to the bar in the corner. Unlike Lincoln's office, this room was small and austere. No artwork hung on the walls, and no ornate tchotchkes decorated the simple wood desk or table. A handmade Terran rug covered the stone floor, adding the only color to the brown room.

"How long have you worked out of this office?" Reyne asked.

"Ever since I became stationmaster. Sixteen years, give or take a few months." Seda looked around before handing Reyne a glass. "I know it could use a decorator's touch, but it works fine for me."

"Hm." Reyne accepted the drink. "I can see why you and Vym are friends. You remind me of what she might have been like in her forties."

"There's *no one* like Vym Patel." Seda took his seat. "Once we free Critch, the Citadel will raise the threat level. When we return to take down the prison, any mistake will be costly."

"Then we'd better not make any mistakes."

Seda gave a small nod. "So when are we heading into the Citadel?"

"In one hour. My team is already in place."

He downed his whiskey in a single gulp. "Then we'd better get going."

CHAPTER 11

SOLITARY RUN

REYNE, Sixx, Boden, and Birk were going up against the Collective's highest security prison with only the crew of the *Honorless* and Seda, and ten of his hired guns, for support. Twenty men suddenly felt like a pitiful match when Reyne saw the Citadel. The structure was a stone fort so large it disappeared deep into the twilight. Every twenty feet or so stood a titanium pillar. Automated drones armed with photon guns perched in chargers at the top of every pillar. An open plain of rocky ground surrounded the Citadel, with no trees or structures to offer camouflage. Whoever had built the Citadel was a very smart person.

Reyne glanced at his wrist comm and watched the blinking dot that represented Critch. The dot hadn't moved for the last ten minutes, and he guessed the man had been locked in his cell for the night. He had no way of knowing where Chutt was, if the man was even still alive, so he figured they could rescue him when they freed the entire Citadel. Besides, Reyne wasn't in as much of a hurry to rescue the pirate who'd so callously killed Doc after finding out she'd betrayed the torrents.

They needed Critch's intel before they risked taking down the Citadel, assuming Critch had what they needed.

Retrieving Critch wouldn't be easy. Escape attempts were common, and Seda had assured them that as long as they made the rescue with a rudimentary approach and tools, they *shouldn't* raise the CUF's suspicion. Assuming Seda was correct, they wouldn't be putting the second part of their plan —freeing everyone inside — at risk.

They waited in a bombed-out house nearest to Critch's location, which was still at least three hundred meters away. They needed to be one hundred meters away for the harpoons to work, but Reyne liked to play it safe, so tonight they were going to get much closer.

Reyne looked across the faces of his men. Sixx sat with a smoothly calm expression, though Reyne worried he was thinking of his wife as much as of the mission. Boden's strong features were tense as he stared straight ahead. Critch's crew remained stoic, but Reyne knew they had to be anxious to retrieve their captain.

Seda and his men also bore cool looks, not a single man fidgeting with his rifle. Reyne trusted his team, but he most certainly did not trust the stationmaster and his team. Over the past day, he'd constantly reconsidered his earlier decision about calling in the specters, but there was no time to wait for them to fly to Terra now.

Reyne checked the time and swallowed before speaking quietly. "It's time. Give a thumbs up if you're good to go."

Each man lifted a thumb. Reyne motioned to his handpicked team of Sixx, Boden, and Birk, leaving everyone else to provide much-needed cover fire from their present location. Reyne's team of four, each carrying a long harpoon gun, hustled over what was left of the house wall and piled into the small hovercraft Sixx had stolen earlier that day. Over the past couple of hours, Boden had been attaching makeshift armor to its body. The team hoped it would be enough to stop photon fire.

Reyne took the driver's seat and laid his harpoon across his lap. He took one final look at the setting sun. The darkness offered no benefit against drones, but it could offer a slight advantage if Reyne and his team were still there when human reinforcements showed up. He looked back across the faces of his team. "Ready for this?"

"Ready, boss," Sixx said without hesitation.

"Ready," Boden and Birk echoed.

Reyne nodded and then accelerated. The hovercraft moved slowly at first, groaning under the excess weight.

"Two hundred meters out," Sixx said after they had driven some distance.

Two drones lit up and lifted from their perches.

"Twelve minutes starts now," Birk added.

"One hundred meters out," Sixx said.

A drone fired a warning shot. The next instant it was shot out of the air by a photon blast from the team behind them. The second drone was destroyed before the first one hit the ground.

Soon after, Sixx said, "Fifty meters."

Drones erupted from across the wall, answered by a cacophony of return gunfire from the support team.

"Twenty meters. Bingo."

Reyne yanked the hovercraft to a stop, turning it parallel to the prison. All four men jumped out and crouched behind the safety of the reinforced hovercraft. They leveled their harpoon guns on the preprogrammed target.

Drones moved in and shot at them, and sparks burned his skin. Just as Reyne suspected, they were in over their heads, his support team's barrage drawing the attention of the drones. As

Reyne had hoped, the drones deemed live gunfire more of a threat than men standing near the Citadel.

"Eleven minutes," Birk said without looking up from his wrist comm.

"Fire when ready," Reyne commanded. The men stood and four *thoomps* were heard in quick succession as four harpoons flew toward the wall. Each hit its mark, forming a square in the stone. Smaller harpoons shot out from each harpoon, resembling giant metal spiders.

"Three, two, one, *now*," Reyne ordered. He hit a button on his gun, and all four harpoons exploded, sending rock and debris flying.

The drones must've recalculated Reyne's team as the greater threat once the harpoons were fired, because they reversed directions and flew toward the four men.

Reyne tossed his harpoon gun. "Into the craft now!"

The drones were now firing nonstop at Reyne's team while the support team fired nonstop at the drones. Drones dropped from the air, only to be replaced by new drones arriving from within the Citadel.

Ducking, they each piled into the hovercraft between close shots.

"I'm hit," Birk called out. "Don't worry. Nothing critical."

Several larger drones emerged from the walls of the Citadel. Whereas the others had single photon rifles, the new drones came armed with full photon arrays.

Reyne drove the hovercraft toward the Citadel's wall. As the dust cleared, he could make out a shape jumping through the freshly made hole. The man in a drab gray uniform landed on the ground and weaved through gunfire. A drone dove at Critch, who knelt and held out something in his hand. Lights on the drone blinked out and the automaton fell the last few feet to the ground.

Reyne sped toward him, and Sixx threw open a door in time for Critch to dive onto Sixx's lap.

Sixx yanked the door shut just as a drone fired into it. "Yow. That's hot," Sixx exclaimed.

A blast burned a hole through the armor plate covering the windshield. The large drone facing off against them lined up to fire again, but a shot from behind knocked the drone to the side, skewing its next shot. It watched them momentarily, and then zoomed away in the direction of their support team.

Reyne spun the hovercraft around and accelerated as fast as the bloated craft could go.

"Ten minutes," Birk said, handing Critch a bag containing clothes, boots, and weapons.

In return, Critch dropped a micro-EMP covered in dry blood into Birk's open palm. "Souvenir."

Boden tapped on the window. "Seems like we're no longer the primary threat. All the drones are going after the gunfire. Our guys are doing their job."

Sixx shoved Critch off him. "My god, you smell awful."

"I didn't have time to shower for our date tonight," Critch snapped back.

"Uh oh. We've got droms joining the party," Boden called out.

Reyne snapped around to see a CUF patrol craft speeding toward them and two more patrol craft speeding toward their support team. *Impossible.*

"I don't understand. My timer is working right," Birk said. "We still have ten minutes on the clock."

"I think someone's playing against us," Reyne gritted out.

An explosion in the distance was followed by incessant gunfire.

"Our guys are taking a beating back there," Sixx said.

"They're gaining on us," Boden announced.

"You're driving like an old lady," Critch said.

"You want to drive?" Reyne countered.

"Yes."

"Well, you can't."

"They're just about on us," Boden called out.

An explosion rocked the hovercraft, and Reyne temporarily lost control. By the time he righted the vehicle, Boden whistled. "Someone on our team had a mini-cannon. I didn't know anyone had those anymore."

"Chutt had one," Critch said as he peeled off the cloned skin that had disguised his scarred face. "He doesn't need it anymore."

No one spoke after that.

Reyne drove down the road and stopped at an abandoned shed. Everyone toppled out of the limping hovercraft and migrated behind the shed and toward their getaway vehicle, a larger—and also stolen—hovercraft. Once inside, Reyne sent a message to Critch's team still with Seda. He grabbed the wheel and headed away from Rebus Station, careful to not speed or drive erratically.

Critch quickly changed his clothes and then sat in the seat next to Reyne. As he pulled on his boots, he spoke. "Thanks for coming. I was going to hit my beacon tonight."

The words were quiet, but Reyne acknowledged them with slight nod. "I'd rather be early than late. The rest of your crew is taking a separate route to the rendezvous point."

Reyne drove for a bit before glancing over at Critch. "Did you really volunteer to get arrested?"

He gave a small nod. "It was a solid plan at the time, but once we got inside, it turned out to be...more complicated than I expected. I recognized many faces, but they've changed so much." He held up a loose flap of cloned skin. "Of course they didn't recognize me. Vym didn't even recognize me."

"So she's still alive?"

"Yeah, but she doesn't look too good." He paused. "We have to get all of them out of there."

"Did you get what we need to do that?"

Critch nodded. "Yes, and I passed around the word to be ready. I told them Drake Fender was coming for his torrents."

Reyne tilted his head. "You think they'll fight again?"

"Some have died. Some have given up. Some have gone crazy; others have gone feral. But most have never stopped fighting."

"We'll get them out of there. First we're going to have to deal with Seda."

Critch frowned. "You think he played us?"

"The CUF arrived within two minutes of the alarm. Do you really think three squads were driving out of town and in the general vicinity of the Citadel at that time of day?"

His features hardened. "Not a chance."

Critch pulled out a small chain from the bag Birk had handed him and slid it over his head. Reyne knew the chain bore a small rilon charm. He knew because he wore one, too. Every torrent wore one.

It was the torrent teardrop.

The small, simple symbol that could be mistaken as a raindrop from the eversea was the culmination of three ideological components of the rebellion. Water represented the torrent army, the teardrop itself represented the struggle the fringe faced under the Collective, and rilon represented the indestructible torrent spirit.

Reyne wore his teardrop with great pride.

When they reached a rock quarry, Reyne pulled into the small parking lot and stopped under a sign that read FAULK INDUSTRIES.

He frowned. "I see business has been good for Seda. I didn't realize he owned the quarries now. That means he's probably got eyes on us right now."

"I take it the RP's in the tunnels?" Critch asked.

"We're supposed to meet back in the colony. I'm changing the plans." He scanned the area, his gaze settling on the office to see any sign of cameras. "Let's get to the tunnels."

They hurried through the darkness until they reached the entrance to the tunnels located on the other side of the quarry. There, Reyne looked over his shoulder one last time, half expecting the CUF to be right behind them.

With his jaw set hard, he stepped inside the old mining tunnels, and the walls seemed to close in, threatening to suffocate him. The dusty smell, cooler temperatures, and stony echoes brought Reyne back to the months he'd lived within the mountain. With Critch at his side, he felt like the same marshal he'd been two decades ago...just with more aches and pains.

Everyone except Critch carried a flashlight, and the lights danced off the stone and beams as they walked.

"They haven't changed much in twenty years," Reyne said, clutching his flashlight in a death grip as he made the first turn. "I checked them out yesterday."

Critch spoke. "Funny how some things stay burned in memory. I think I could still get around these tunnels with my eyes closed."

"I think I could, too," Reyne said.

They walked in silence, their steps echoing down the caverns.

"You call that a gunshot? You're not even bleeding," Sixx said from behind them.

"I said it wasn't critical," Birk replied.

Reyne glanced back to see Birk holding up his hand, with the tip of his pinky finger now missing. He smirked.

"I think you'll survive," Critch said.

"Damn it, I told you guys it wasn't critical," Birk said once again, then added quietly, "But it sure does hurt."

Critch's humor was all too brief as his gaze returned to the direction they'd come from. "I got what I needed, but the cost was too high on this one." After a brief pause, he spoke again. "I'm going to make sure it was worth it by getting every last person out of there."

CHAPTER 12

CHOOSING SIDES

CRITCH'S CREW—EVEN Gabe—welcomed their captain back as soon as they caught up with him and Reyne's team in the tunnels.

Maddox, one of Critch's crew, sobered soon after greeting his captain. "We lost Sam. But at least he never felt a thing."

Critch grimaced. "Damn it. Not Sam."

Maddox paused. "What's the word on Chutt?"

Critch's jaw clenched. "He didn't make it."

Silence befell his crew.

Maddox turned to Reyne. "Why the sudden change in RP?"

Before Reyne could answer, the sounds of approaching steps had everyone rushing to level their pistols and rifles on the entrance. Moments later, Seda and his men stepped into the underground room. Their eyes widened, and Seda's men raised their weapons in defense.

"Funny," Seda said. "I was beginning to feel like you were having a party and I wasn't invited." He looked at Reyne. "You changed the rendezvous location without telling me. At least you were nice enough to stop at one of my businesses so my security could report your location to me."

Reyne strode right up to the stationmaster and slammed him into the wall.

Seda shoved him off and had him pinned to the same wall in a flash of movement. "Watch yourself. Assaulting me is becoming an unpleasant habit of yours."

Reyne glared. "How'd the CUF get there so soon, Seda?"

Seda's eyes narrowed before he pushed away from Reyne. "We had a leak. I plugged it."

"How convenient," Reyne said.

"If I was going to betray you, I'd wait until everyone was in the same room and then gas it. I don't like risking my life and the lives of my men if I don't have to. Tipping off the CUF got three good men killed today."

One of Critch's crew—Alex was his name—holstered his pistol and held up a hand. "Let's all just put our weapons away and talk." He looked at Reyne. "Seda's telling the truth. I saw what happened back at the Citadel. One of Seda's guys sold us out. Seda caught on and drifted him."

Seda held out a hand as he explained. "Donovan gave himself away when Vlad got shot by one of the patrols that hit us at the Citadel. Don always had a lousy poker face. He'd been with me a long time. He was a very capable soldier, but greedy. I thought I paid him enough to satisfy his itch. I was wrong, and Vlad and Sam paid the price for Donovan's treachery. It was Donovan who tipped off the CUF to make a few extra credits. What he didn't expect was seeing his pal have his brains blown out by a dromadier, and it threw him."

Critch then walked between the two groups. "It's done. Holster your weapons *now*. We don't have time for this. We have work to do."

Everyone obeyed.

Seda smoothed his shirt and walked over to Critch. "It's nice to see you made it," Seda said. "Did you see Stationmaster Patel during your stay?"

"She's alive, but she needs medical attention."

"Well, then we'd better get her out of there. Do you have the location of the generators?"

Critch pointed to his head. "I need to see a map."

Seda nodded to his men. "Tax, Corbin, cover the entrance. The rest of you, stay sharp." He pulled out a tablet and set it down on a crate. He ran his hands through several command sequences. A projected image of the Citadel displayed on the wall. Seda tapped on the tablet again to zoom in on the image, and the entire facility's layout appeared.

Seda began. "The walls and ceilings are reinforced with titanium, and the floors are solid rock with titanium rebar. As you can see, it's the Collective's largest Faraday cage to prevent any sort of EMP disturbance."

"Cages can be broken," Reyne said.

"It won't be easy," Seda said. "We must use EMPs. Any other tools involve deadly force, which guarantees prisoner deaths from friendly fire as well as draws unwanted attention from the outside."

Critch pulled up a crate and sat down. "EMPs will work." He traced his fingers around the walls. "All the cells line the outer walls, so we can't shoot our way in without collateral damage. Prisoners are randomly rotated into new cells each day, so it's impossible to know where anyone is on any given day. To make it more complicated, prisoners are rotated between two shifts. When one shift is in the commons, the other shift is in cells."

Critch continued. "That the Citadel is fully automated will work in our favor. I only saw two staff when I was there. The drones distribute food and supplies. They shock anyone carrying more than one food ration or anything else they deem to be on the contraband list. Other than that, it's a self-run ecosystem. The problem within the prison is the people. The gangs control everything. While the majority are political prisoners, there are some criminals in there. I don't see a way to separate the two when we take down the Citadel."

Reyne's lips thinned. "We'll be unleashing criminals back into the fringe. I hadn't thought of that."

"I have," Seda said. "I have no qualms about releasing criminals back into the system if it means we're doing a greater good."

"I figure we make the same offer to everyone, regardless of why they're in there," Critch said as he scrolled through the maps. "Become a torrent or go their own way. But we'll be quite clear: any torrent who breaks the rules will pay the price."

"They'll naturally congregate with their gangs from the Citadel after we free them," Reyne said. "We'll likely have to deal with that at some point."

"Any thug who tries to return to his previous ways on my planet will find swift justice from me," Seda said.

"Here they are," Critch said and both men turned to the screen. "The backup generators are here and"—he shifted the map— "here, across the prison."

Seda frowned. "They have two separate backup generators? That complicates things."

Critch continued. "The Citadel has redundancies for everything. So it makes sense it has redundant backup systems. It's a simple layout once you understand it. If you cut the Citadel down the middle, each half is a mirror image of the other. The generators sit a level below the open prison area where prisoners spend each day, and each is enclosed in its own Faraday cage to protect it from EMPs and electrical interference."

Reyne held up three fingers. "We need *three* EMP teams.

Two teams to take down the generators and a team to take down the Citadel."

"I believe you could still get by with two teams," Seda offered. "A team for each generator. Then, once the generators are fried, one of the teams sets off the big EMP."

Critch turned to Birk. "How far out are the specters? We could use some of them on this one."

"They're all at Nova Colony," Birk answered. "To assist with the evacuations."

Critch frowned. "Evacuations from what?"

"The CUF has been using the Coast for target practice," Reyne said.

"I can call them in if we need them," Birk offered.

Critch held up a hand. "No. They can do more good there."

"I have plenty of staff," Seda offered. "I've been planning this mission for quite some time."

"It'll have to do." Critch tapped the map. "I had a plan to bring down the Citadel while we were inside, but it fell through. Chutt was collecting supplies when he got caught."

"The drones?" Reyne asked.

Critch shook his head. "A gang. Led by a former torrent, no less. Mingh didn't take kindly to Chutt stealing from their stash, even if it was to break them out."

"Mingh?" Reyne recalled the torrent and his love for killing dromadiers. "That one always had a mean streak."

Critch's voice lowered. "I'm looking forward to getting payback when this is over."

"You'll find him."

Critch remained silent.

Reyne changed the subject. "The EMP teams are the easy part. We have to prevent their alarms from sounding before we set off the EMPs. Otherwise, the CUF will be able to pick off escapees faster than using automatic blasters on vigs. The injured and weak ones, like Vym, won't stand a chance."

"The alarms are automated," Critch said. "It only takes a single drone to fire off the call to the CUF and we're fighting our way out."

"Don't worry. I've had that part worked out for some time," Seda said, rubbing his chin. "The drones will think our teams are all prison staff."

"How so?" Reyne asked.

"The staff wears vests. Otherwise, the drones don't seem to even care who's who in there," Seda replied. "Coincidentally, the vests were made at one of my facilities in Rebus Station." He continued analyzing the maps. "The staff are collocated in the northwest corner, here. As you can see, they have their own entrance. Our teams go in through there and gas the entire section to neutralize any staff."

"We don't know how smart the systems are," Critch said. "We'll have to keep our teams small in case large numbers trigger warnings."

"Okay," Reyne began. "We send in two teams through the staff entrance. They knock out the staff and make their way through the lower levels to the generators. Each team fries the generators, then one sets off a large EMP within the prison itself."

Seda nodded. "Then we have all the time in the world to transport the freed prisoners from there to Broken Mountain."

Reyne and Critch both flinched.

"Broken Mountain?" Reyne asked.

"The tunnels in Broken Mountain were destroyed," Critch said in a monotone.

"They were," Seda said. "To the Collective, my quarries aren't my most profitable companies. What they don't know is that my quarries do much more than produce gravel. For the past ten years, I've had teams clearing out the tunnels. About a third of them have been rebuilt to date. There's enough space to hide everyone, and the CUF would never think of looking there."

"Of course they wouldn't." Critch pushed to his feet. "You know how many torrents were slaughtered there? For many of those torrents wasting away in the Citadel, the last thing they saw before prison walls was the CUF invading Broken Mountain."

Memories of the past had Reyne's heart beating faster. "The torrents inside may still be shell-shocked from Broken Mountain. That might not be the best place. It will push some over the edge."

"We could bring in the *Matador*," Critch offered. "It could hold everyone."

"Impossible," Seda said. "You can't bring a supply ship of that size onto Terra without drawing the attention of every CUF ship in the quadrant. It'll get blown out of the sky."

A chime sounded, and Seda glanced down at his pocket.

Reyne eyed Seda. "That's your *other* tablet. You'd better answer it."

Seda stood. "Excuse me. Let's take a brief break."

Reyne shook his head. "No. Anyone who's not Critch, Seda, or me, leave the room."

Seda narrowed his gaze onto Reyne. "What are you doing?"

"Take it here." Reyne motioned to the crate Seda had been sitting on. "You're either for the torrents or you're for the Collective. What will it be?"

Seda pursed his lips for a moment, and then he waved off his men. "You heard him. Everyone out."

The stationmaster reclaimed his seat with a sigh and pulled out the tablet from his pant pocket.

Upon seeing the dark gray device, Critch's lips parted. "You're a Founder."

Seda spoke. "I made my choice long ago, but there are delicate matters involved. I require your absolute silence and trust."

"Done," Reyne quickly stated.

Seda went through a series of keystrokes, and his face lost any hint of emotion before he spoke into the tablet. "Accept call."

Reyne and Critch sat facing Seda, watching him watch his tablet.

"I just learned of some interesting news on Terra."

Reyne's blood ran cold. He shot a glance at Critch, whose angry expression and clenched fists made it clear he also recognized the voice. Mason.

"What news would that be?" Seda asked.

"I saw images of three men who were killed outside the Citadel during a prison break tonight. Two of them were your employees."

"Yes, they worked for me," Seda replied. "However, they were freelancing at the time—as do all my employees from time to time. That pair obviously could've shown better taste in their extracurricular activities."

"Obviously."

Reyne cringed at the superiority in Mason's voice, and he craved to jump through the tablet and kill the Founder.

"However, what piqued my curiosity was the third corpse. A pirate from the Honorless, *no less. Did you know they were associating with pirates?"*

"As I said, they freelance, and I do not keep tabs on who they choose to associate with. They are not tenured to me and can do what they wish to make money on the side."

"You should care. They were associating with a rather dangerous demographic."

"They were guns for hire. Everyone they associated with is dangerous."

"However, since they worked for you, their choices could reflect poorly on you should that information comes to light."

"I control the Terran news. The only way that information would become known is if it were leaked to the Collective news."

"I'll do my best to see that doesn't happen. Now, tell me about the prisoner that escaped. I believe his name was Eben Abery, Junior."

"I know very little as yet. I ran a search when I learned of my men's involvement. Abery is a low-level criminal with a temper, with two prior arrests for shoplifting. His latest arrest was for assaulting a citizen."

"Yes, I read his story. He seems a waste of Collective resources. I don't see why someone of his low stature would have the assets to arrange a prison break."

"I am looking into it."

"I'm sure you are. However, you realize we are at a precarious time. We must be ever diligent and stand united. I know you felt the death of Seamstress, and I hope that hasn't caused you to waver in your allegiances."

"Never. Just as I hope the loss of Baker hasn't done the same to you."

"The betrayal of a Founder is felt by us all." Each word in Mason's response was clipped and full of anger. *"I trust you to keep me apprised on any torrent activity you learn of."*

"Of course. As always, I trust you to keep me apprised of any significant activity planned in the fringe."

"Of course. For the free."

"For the Founders."

Seda ended the call. He then frowned, the first emotion to cross his face since he took the call. "Mason knows that my men would never take any side jobs without my approval," he said without looking up, and began typing out a message on the same gray tablet.

Critch grimaced. "How can you handle talking with him, knowing the crimes he's committed?"

Seda still didn't look up. "Because I have to."

Critch cracked his knuckles. "I look forward to breaking that man's neck."

Seda held up a hand to silence Critch and continued typing. Finished, he slid the tablet into his pant pocket.

Seda leveled a hard gaze on them. "Everything has changed. If Mason knows I'm working with torrents, he's no doubt deduced that I initiated the new rebellion. He will quickly move against me."

"Watch yourself," Critch said. "Vym initiated the Uprising, and she engaged me to help her. Don't take credit for her years of hard work. Besides, I don't see you wearing one of these." He lifted the chain to reveal the torrent teardrop.

"Except that Vym's also a Founder." Reyne narrowed his gaze on Seda. "If you're the one she's been working with all this time, that makes you Aeronaut. So you're the Founder overseeing every major event that happens in the colonies. No wonder Mason speaks directly with you. I didn't expect that, but it makes perfect sense that Aeronaut would be one of the most powerful men in the fringe. You and Mason play with lives like they're game pieces."

"Mason enjoys playing games. I've never found much pleasure in them." Seda held up his hands. "Enough small talk. We need to move against the Citadel tonight, and then I must focus on minimizing whatever havoc Mason has planned."

"You're going to get me in front of Mason," Critch said.

"Killing Mason will only speed up the plans he's set in motion. Taking him down requires finesse, something that's far better aligned to my skills than yours, I believe."

"I will have retribution."

"We'll all have retribution," Reyne said. "Mason—Gabriel Heid—will be stopped."

"But tonight we free Vym and everyone else in the Citadel," Seda said.

"We'll need to prep the teams," Reyne said. "I'll call Throttle and have her prep the ships. If Mason is about to make a move, we'd better be ready for a hasty retreat."

"I'll send Gabe up to help," Critch added.

"I'll have the necessary supplies delivered to the quarry," Seda said. "However, I must caution both of you against leading teams into the Citadel."

Both men guffawed.

"As visible torrent leaders, you need to stay alive. I have capable officers under my command to lead the infiltration teams."

Critch chuckled. "If you don't get why we're heading in, you don't understand what it means to be a torrent leader. Leading from the shadows isn't leading at all."

Reyne nodded. "We're both going in."

Seda pursed his lips. "I assumed you wouldn't be swayed. I'll have someone bring cloning gel for Reyne's skin. I'm sorry, but you can't enter the Citadel without a disguise. Even a disguise may not be enough for any who knew you well."

Reyne inhaled deeply. "I know." He walked over to the crates. He disconnected a rifle from the automated tracking swivel base, which was still homed in on the beacon Reyne had planted earlier. He slung the rifle over his shoulder. "Let's head out."

Seda had been watching Reyne, and his lips parted when realization struck. He took off his jacket and began scrutinizing it. After a moment of searching, he plucked something off it. He tossed the tiny tracker back to Reyne. "So that's why you grabbed me earlier. This entire time, all you had to do was press a button, and I was a dead man."

Reyne stuck the track back into its storage slot on the swivel base. "At the time, I didn't trust you."

Seda's brow rose. "Now you do, I hope."

"I'm getting closer."

CHAPTER 13

CAGED POWER

REYNE MASSAGED HIS FACE, trying to make the cloned skin over his real skin tingle less.

"Itches, doesn't it?" Critch asked. "It eventually quits feeling like bugs crawling on you and more like bugs just sitting on you. Give it a day or so."

Reyne frowned at him. "This mission will be over in six hours."

Critch shrugged.

"We're approaching the entrance and no drones have come alive yet," Boden announced from the front seat of their repainted hovercraft. "Seda was right about the CUF logo serving as a free pass."

When a door in the side of the building opened, allowing them to drive inside, Reyne tapped his comm. "Seda, we're heading inside. We'll notify you once we're in position. Keep your eyes and ears open out there and be ready with the transports."

"*Copy that,*" Seda's response came through Reyne's earpiece.

"All right, everyone," Critch said. "Check your earpieces to make sure you're reading me. Remember that these earpieces are programmed so that transmissions go out to everyone wearing them. That means keep chatter to a minimum. Make sure you have your gas masks. I don't need any of you falling asleep on the job."

"Set your weapons to 'stun'," Reyne added. "We don't want to kill any prisoners."

"Unless they intend to kill you. Then, by all means, kill them," Critch said.

Reyne frowned at his fellow captain, but Critch was looking out the window. His body was taut with tension, and Reyne knew his compatriot was already back inside the Citadel. Reyne became worried. If a week inside that prison haunted a man like Critch, what kinds of mental states would the other prisoners be in?

The vehicle stopped and they all stepped out, wearing the black torrent fatigues Seda had provided. In the dark, they could nearly pass as dromadiers, who wore blue suits.

Reyne's team was composed of Sixx, Boden, and Maddox—a member of Critch's crew. Critch's team included Birk, Nat, and Grundy—all from his crew.

He noticed a scanner off to their right, and its red eye ran over each vest in quick succession. A second later, an automated voice said, *"Welcome to the Citadel. For your safety, wear your vest at all times. Should you need support or directions, please proceed to the nearest terminal."*

From where they stood in the receiving bay, there was a single large door straight ahead. Birk and Nat moved around the back of the vehicle they'd come in and lifted out a large metal box.

"Make sure it's good and grounded," Critch ordered. "We don't want to risk frying it."

"We've got it, captain," Nat said.

When the pair rejoined their group, both teams moved toward the door, which opened when they drew near. Once through, Sixx swung off his satchel and pulled out a handful of silver orbs.

"Hello. We weren't expecting company tonight."

Reyne looked up to see a man heading down the steps toward them. He was wearing civilian clothes and had pale skin, as if he hadn't been outside in months.

Alex, from Critch's crew, stepped forward. "We were assigned to run audits on your systems."

The man leaned against the railing. "I don't understand. We passed the audit last month. Why another one so soon?"

Alex shrugged. "Who knows what's going on. All I know is our workload has tripled all of a sudden with random audits. You know the CUF. If there's one thing they're good at, it's red tape."

The man rolled his eyes. "And spending taxpayer dollars. You need any help from me?"

"Nope," Alex replied. "It looks like we should be out of your hair in a few hours."

"I'll be off shift by then, so if I'm not around, just ask for Ginny if you need anything." The man waved and started to walk away, and then paused. "Oh, wait. You'll need the master key. Hold on." He jogged up the stairs.

Reyne noticed several hands resting on their holsters, and he swallowed, hoping no one got twitchy.

The man reappeared and held out a small card before dropping it down. Alex caught it. "Thanks, buddy. Should I just leave it with Ginny when we're through?"

"Yeah, that's great. Thanks." With that, the man disappeared.

When Alex turned to face Reyne and the others, he seemed as surprised as Reyne felt. "That was easier than I expected. I guess civilians working for the CUF are a bit more laid back than the CUF."

"I don't think these guys get much company," Sixx said. "I'm guessing no one ever comes here who isn't either in cuffs or under orders to be here."

Alex swiped the card over the scanner, and it came to life. *"Master key detected."*

"Computer, we're running tests on your air and power systems. Your sensors will pick up anomalies. Disregard all anomalies in those systems for the next eight hours."

"Confirmed. Power systems and air systems will be set in test mode until 0420."

"Gas masks, everyone," Critch said.

"These are handy little things." Alex waved the keycard before he slid it into his pocket. "Much easier than coaxing a hardheaded system into playing nice."

Sixx glanced around to make sure everyone had their gas masks on. "Showtime." He tossed the orbs into the air, where they floated, and he hurriedly slid on his mask. "Three, two, one." His countdown came out muffled through his mask.

The orbs disintegrated, and a white haze shot out in all directions.

"Set your timers," Sixx said. "Nine minutes until the air clears, starting now."

Reyne checked the time on his comm before looking at Critch.

Critch nodded. "We'll see you back here." He motioned for his team, and they took off at a quick walk down the stairs.

Critch's team was taking the generators on the other side of the prison and would need at least an extra thirty minutes to walk the distance through the lower levels. Since Reyne's team was responsible for taking down the nearby generators, he had the additional task of making sure the staff had all succumbed to the gas before they set off any alarms.

Reyne motioned to his team, and Sixx took the lead up the

stairs, with Boden right behind him. Maddox covered their rear. Sixx's temperament had become less lighthearted and far more sullen and straightforward since the meeting with Lincoln. Reyne knew the man was pretending that everything was fine, when in fact he was fighting an internal battle to stay here with the crew and not run back to Devil Town to squeeze Lincoln for information.

Sixx stopped outside the first room they reached on the next level, which turned out to be the computer room. Through the glass door, Reyne recognized the tech who'd greeted him. The man now lay sprawled on the floor, having not even made it back to his desk before Sixx released the gas. They continued down the hall, finding individual quarters lining the walls. Small windows on each door confirmed that the staff—nine in total— were all down.

Reyne transmitted to all the teams. "Staff are confirmed down."

"*Received,*" came Critch's voice.

Seda's voice soon followed with "*copy that.*"

Satisfied, Reyne's team made their way back down to the main level, then down another flight to the level where the backup generators would be. So far, it felt like they were in an office building rather than a prison, since he'd yet to see a single cell, let alone a prisoner. In fact, the only sign that they were in a prison at all was the drones perched near the ceilings in perfectly spaced lengths.

Sixx's wrist comm beeped. "Looks like our nine minutes are up." He slid off his gas mask and breathed in the air. Then he turned and gave the others a thumbs up. "Not the freshest air down here, but more comfortable than wearing a mask."

They each removed their masks and hooked them onto their belts. Sixx continued to lead the way, using the map on his comm to guide them through the tunnels. They walked slowly but with purpose so that their movements triggered no attention from the drones.

"They could use a cleaning crew," Sixx muttered as he brushed away a cobweb. "One last turn up ahead."

A few seconds later, as they made a turn, a set of machines came into view. The backup generators were larger than most primary generators. They were bulbous, red metal monsters humming quietly along as they sat within a thick cage of metal bars.

"What a waste of titanium," Boden said.

Maddox shook his head. "The real waste is letting them idle. Burning juice just to have them ready to power the prison in a second rather than in several seconds."

Reyne nodded. "Let's get prepped."

Boden and Maddox pulled off the bags they each carried and carefully removed the contents. Inside each bag was an EMP bomb and detonator, though Maddox's was several times the size of Boden's.

Maddox chuckled. "Let me guess. She said size doesn't matter and you believed her."

Boden shot the other man a wry glance as he continued assembling his EMP. He plugged the wire detonator into the bomb and slid the device through an opening in the cage. He unraveled the wire and held up the detonator. "Armed and ready."

Maddox, who'd also been working on his bomb, climbed to his feet, standing over the larger device. "Big Betty here is also armed and ready to go."

Reyne nodded before transmitting to everyone, "Team North is in position and ready."

"Team Rebus is ready to take the entrances," Seda replied.

Several seconds later, Critch's voice came through. *"Hold on. Team South needs another minute."* He sounded out of breath, and Reyne wondered what they had encountered on their journey across the prison's underbelly.

They waited. Every few seconds, Reyne found himself eying the nearest drone, expecting it to light up and sound the alarms, but it never moved. After a minute, Reyne's heart was pounding and his palms were sweaty. After another minute, he transmitted again. "Team South, what's your status?"

No response.

He frowned and looked across his team's faces. Everyone looked impatient, and Maddox looked worried. When Critch's rushed voice finally came through their earpieces, Reyne jumped.

"Team South is in position and ready. Discharge generators in six, five, four, three, two, one. Now."

Reyne kept his eyes on Boden during the entire sequence and watched him depress the detonator. The peculiar thing about EMP bombs was that they gave no visual or audible cue that they'd been detonated. There was no boom, no bright flash, nothing. The only sign the EMP had worked was that the constant humming of the generator suddenly faded to silence.

"Team South reports successful discharge. Ready for full discharge."

"Team North reports successful discharge and is ready for full," Reyne said.

"Team Rebus is ready to discharge on your count," Seda transmitted.

Reyne turned to watch Maddox. "Discharging in six, five, four, three, two, one. Now."

Maddox pressed the detonator. The lights went out, blanketing them in darkness. Critch's team would've discharged a large EMP bomb at the same moment as a redundancy, and it was clear at least one bomb worked. Outside, Seda had released an EMP across the entire fringe station to fry local CUF systems and cause chaos.

Reyne dropped the now-useless earpiece and pulled out several glow sticks from his pocket. He cracked them and handed one out to each of his team. He flashed the light at a drone and relaxed when it showed no signs of activity.

"Let's get upstairs to hook up with Team South," he said. Without waiting for a response, he began jogging back the way they'd come. His joints protested the beating of his boots against the concrete, but adrenaline and anxiety helped him ignore them.

He turned the corner and kept going. His wrist comm had been fried during the EMP, and so they had no maps. But Reyne's memory was as good as ever, and he recalled every turn they'd made until they found themselves back on the main level.

There, Sixx and Maddox went to work manually opening the door that led outside while Boden knelt at the metal box they'd left near the vehicle and powered up the equipment. He looked over his shoulder. "Everything's in the green. We're good."

"Good. Now we wait," Reyne said.

Once the two men had the outer door open, they moved to the inner entrance that led to the prison area. Sixx spoke. "Whoever designed this must've figured the prison would never be without power. It has no manual locking mechanisms."

"So you can get it open?" Reyne asked.

"A baby could get it open."

Reyne watched as Sixx and Maddox cut whatever cables they deemed necessary, and soon climbed to their feet.

"Ready whenever you are," Sixx said.

"We wait for Team South." The waiting was near unbearable as they lingered in the receiving area for Critch's team to return. Reyne could hear human activity growing within the prison area, and he knew Seda would have the main entrance open by now.

"They sound like they're tearing the place apart," Maddox said.

With every scream and shout he heard, Reyne craved to

launch the contents of the crate. However, if they opened the inner door to release the system before Reyne's and Critch's teams were ready to leave, the teams could be swallowed in a sea of fleeing escapees.

Reyne tossed a hurried glance at Boden. "We give them five more minutes before we launch."

With his comm now offline, Reyne had no timer, so he guessed. When he reached what seemed to be three minutes, he heard the sounds of boot steps running up the stairs. He grabbed his pistol, but holstered it as soon as he confirmed it was Critch and his team. Wet sheens covered their faces, and they were breathing heavily.

"About time," Reyne said. Without further acknowledgement, he turned to Boden. "Power it up." He then pointed to the prison area's entrance. "Open it up."

Sixx and Maddox slid the door open and jumped out of the way as several prisoners toppled through. When the escapees climbed to their feet, their wide gazes scanned the room, and then they barreled past Sixx and Maddox as they fled outside.

"You're safe now," Reyne called out after them. "Head to the transports."

He had no idea if they'd listened, because they'd already run outside and disappeared around the wall.

A glow filled the room as the drones in the metal case shot to life and flew through the doorway and into the prison area. Reyne stood and watched as tiny light pellets began to fill the prison, lighting it up with thousands of miniscule stars. A gentle automated voice blared out from the drones' speakers.

"The Citadel is being shut down, courtesy of the torrent army. Make your way to the central entrances where transports wait to bring you to safety. Move in a steady but cautious manner to the transports. We ask that you please assist anyone who may not be

able to get to the transports on their own. You are safe. You do not need to hide or run away."

The message repeated as the drones flew around the prison, lighting the way to the entrances.

More and more prisoners began to pour through the doorway nearest Reyne and shoved their way outside.

"We need to get out of here!" Critch yelled, and Reyne couldn't agree more. He made sure his team was still with him, then joined the wave of foul-smelling humans. Once outside, the people seemed to scatter rather than head toward the transports, which he had expected but was still disappointed to see. They looked like rats fleeing a sinking ship.

The eight torrents stood in silence as everyone else rabbited around them. Critch came to stand at Reyne's side.

"I was beginning to worry about you," Reyne said.

"Nothing we couldn't handle. When I was a prisoner, I couldn't get through all the passageways without getting zapped by one of those wasps flying around all the time. I didn't know that there was a fire door midway down the tunnel that they keep locked. We had to move through the general population, which slowed us down."

"Any of them attack you?"

Critch chuckled. "I wasn't wearing a disguise this time. You'd have thought I was some kind of god the way they all threw themselves at me." He stared out into the night and sighed. "It's chaos out here."

Reyne looked across the barren fields, with thousands of shapes—all wearing gray prison garb—running in every direction. A significant number were walking in relatively ordered lines to the procession of EMP-shielded, dark-painted buses Seda had arranged.

In the distance, Rebus Station stood dark since Seda had detonated a massive EMP in the area to serve as a distraction.

A bullet-shaped cruiser zoomed toward them, scattering prisoners out of its path. The hovercraft slid to a stop, and a door opened to reveal a frowning Seda. "Get in. We've got a problem."

As everyone piled into the craft, Reyne asked, "What's the problem?"

"Mason has made his first move," Seda answered. "There's a squadron of CUF gunships entering Terra's orbit right now, and every single one of them are on a direct path to the Citadel."

CHAPTER 14

GHOST SHIPS

"THE GUNSHIPS WILL SLAUGHTER EVERYONE," Reyne said. "Without heavy ground-to-air artillery, we don't stand a chance against them from the ground."

"We need to get to our ships," Critch said. "We can draw their attention away from the people."

"There's no time," Seda said, jackknifing the cruiser upward and speeding away in the night sky. "It would take you an hour to get to your ships. I can get to mine in three minutes."

Reyne looked to the sky, still not seeing the incoming ships. He turned around to check on Boden and Sixx to find each sitting silently in the seats next to Critch's crew. It was the first time in days that Sixx didn't look like his mind was somewhere else. It only took the threat of a gunship squadron to bring him back, Reyne thought humorlessly. In the hovercraft, everyone's eyes were wide and bodies tense, which was exactly how Reyne suspected he looked. After all, there was only one thing you did if a squadron of gunships was headed your way. Run.

Seconds felt like minutes as Seda's cruiser shot through the sky, breaking the sound barrier with popping sounds.

"You have a gunship?" Critch asked.

"No."

"Then it's no match against the CUF."

The cruiser slowed and descended sharply as they approached a tall hill illuminated by the planet's two moons. Reyne stiffened as they closed the distance to the hill. He didn't breathe until the cruiser skimmed over the ground and then flew in parallel to the incline.

"You're close enough I could reach out and pick a few flowers," Critch said drily.

Reyne's muscles cramped from tension. "You're going too fast."

Seda made no adjustment.

He grabbed the seat as the ground grew closer and closer. "Seda."

"Trust me."

"Still working on that," Reyne said.

"Seda," Critch joined in.

Someone in the backseat yelled just as the cruiser met the ground.

The cruiser then flew *through* the ground, to be more accurate.

"A hologram." Reyne deflated. "You could've told us."

Seda smiled.

Below the hologram, a long runway stood. A single hangar that could easily hold the entire fleet of specters stood at one end. What drew Reyne's attention and sounds of awe throughout the cruiser was the spacecraft powered up nearby that dwarfed the hangar.

"You have a warship," Critch said incredulously.

Reyne's eyes narrowed as he took in the ship. It was less than half the size of modern warships, but that didn't make it any less threatening. He remembered when the torrents had a fleet of them gliding through space. With smooth lines and an oval hull, she was beautiful. When he made out the name on the side, he smiled. "Not just any warship. It's the *Raptor*."

"Impossible," Critch said. "She was destroyed during the Uprising."

Seda shook his head. "It was only damaged. It didn't burn up in the atmosphere as was rumored."

"I think I'm in love," Boden murmured from the backseat.

"Get ready to move," Seda said. "We need to switch ships without any delay."

Seda brought the cruiser down hard and fast, but slipped it into a softer landing than Reyne had expected. He'd been so nervous during the flight that he'd failed to notice that Seda was an impressive pilot. "How many times have you flown the Coastal Run?" he asked Seda as they left the hovercraft and jogged over to the warship.

"None, officially. A stationmaster would never do something so reckless." Seda grabbed a ladder and started climbing up into the docked ship. Over his shoulder, he added, "Unofficially, seven times."

As they rushed on board, Birk frowned. "It's an antique."

"It's a classic," Critch corrected him as he hurried past him.

As soon as Seda entered the bridge, he called out. "Hari, report."

The woman standing on board turned. "Ready for immediate departure, sir. I've taken the liberty of cycling all gun systems. The *Raptor* is ready."

He buckled in at the captain's helm. "Then let's not sit around here any longer. If this doesn't draw the CUF's attention, nothing will." He glanced back at Reyne and Critch. "Hari and I have the flight controls. I need your teams to handle the weapon systems. Everything's manual on this old girl."

"I remember," Reyne said before facing Critch. "My team will take forward cannons. You take aft."

"Wilco," Critch replied and turned to his crew, "Team South, you're with me."

As they ran off, Reyne said, "Team North, come with me." The three men followed him off the bridge and up a level. He grabbed the railing when the ship lunged forward, and he suspected Seda was using full propulsion to build speed faster.

He pointed to the various gunners' chairs. "Sixx, I want you front and center on the big cannon."

"Hoowee," Sixx hollered with glee as he ran to claim his seat.

"Boden, you take this corner cannon."

"Got it, boss."

He turned to Maddox. "Do you know how to operate phase cannons?"

Maddox lifted his brows as though it was a stupid question.

"Of course you do. How about you take the corner cannon opposite Boden."

Reyne took a step back to make sure his team was buckled in and comfortable with the controls. Assured they all were ready, he sat down in an open gunner's chair and strapped in. Hari had been true to her word, and the systems were already up at one hundred percent. He pulled up the gun's scanner to find several blips moving toward a central location.

"Check your scanners. We've got bogeys screaming in," Reyne called out, and then added, "Remember, cannons are slower than photon guns, so fire only when you have a solid target. That goes double for you, Sixx."

"Yeah, yeah, boss. Got it," Sixx hollered back.

The large warship accelerated more slowly than the cruiser had, but it continued to gain momentum and closed the distance back to the Citadel *nearly* as quickly as the arriving gunships.

However, the gunships would be in firing range of the people on the ground before the *Raptor* could stop them.

Reyne hollered, "Sixx, fire off a shot at the nearest gunship."

"They're not in range yet."

"I know. Just do it. Let's see if we can't draw their attention away from the crowds."

Reyne watched the scanner as more gunships broke through the atmosphere and sped toward the Citadel. His muscles remained taut as he waited for the first shot. If the *Raptor* wasn't enough to draw all the gunships to them, the Citadel would be the site of a massacre.

A minor shockwave rumbled through the *Raptor*, and Reyne saw the system report a shot had been fired. He watched his scanner. No gunships disappeared, not that he'd expect them to get that lucky this far out. However, the ship nearest to them took evasive maneuvers.

"I piqued the curiosity of one of the buggers," Sixx said. "He's changed course and is coming straight at us."

"We have one incoming gunship. We're raising defensive shields," Hari said on the intercom.

Interminable seconds passed, and the remaining ships continued on their path to the Citadel. "Change course, damn it," Reyne muttered to himself, but the gunships ignored his plea.

"I'm reporting shots fired on the Citadel," Hari's voice came through the speaker system.

The CUF had launched their attack, and Reyne felt powerless to stop it. "Can't this thing go any faster?" he wondered aloud.

"It can, but we'd overshoot the Citadel. By the way, your mike is pressed," Hari said.

Reyne glanced down and noticed he was clenching the joystick so tightly he'd had his intercom depressed. He shook his hands, trying to release the tension.

"Bogey at our twelve. Coming in hot. Guess they didn't like my handshake," Sixx announced.

He felt another cannon blast reverberate through the ship. The gunship's icon on the scanner swerved but still didn't disappear, and soon tracked back onto its direct course at the warship, though it began to weave to make itself a harder target.

"You missed," Maddox said.

"I know," Sixx replied. "These old cannons are slower than I expected. I'll get him this time."

Reyne understood Sixx's frustration. Even though Sixx was an expert marksman, cannons weren't like photon guns. They had a limited rotation arc and took longer to adjust than smaller guns. Where it would take a dozen or more photon shots to take out a ship, a single phase cannon blast would blast through shields and knock a ship out of the sky.

After Sixx's second fire, the scanner showed nine other gunships adjust course to come at the *Raptor*, leaving four still on course for the Citadel, and how many more still descending from orbit.

"Looks like we're getting their attention now," Reyne said to himself. Even though every gunner had his own scanner, he tapped his intercom. "Prepare for incoming. The party's getting started."

The first gunship came in fast at the *Raptor*, and Sixx fired at it. The bogey banked at the last second. Multiple blasts came from the warship, and the gunship disappeared off the scanner.

"Got 'em for you, Sixx," Maddox called out.

The incoming gunships were coming in even faster, and the screen indicated they'd be at the warship in twenty seconds.

"Hold on for evasive maneuvers," Seda announced an instant before the ship banked to the left. The movement was slow, with little noticeable G-force, like a whale rolling in the ocean.

Reyne's screen flashed a warning, and he saw multiple incoming shots fired from the ships.

The *Raptor* felt every hit and returned fire. Another icon disappeared off the screen. The remaining ships broke off in a starburst pattern, speeding over and around the warship.

Reyne's cannon was located on the side of the ship, meaning he had the least amount of rotation. He fired and missed.

An explosion off to his right made him duck. He looked to find smoke pouring through a hole midway down the ship. "Hull breach! Don't let these bastards get a bead on us!"

Neither warships nor gunships were designed for in-gravity combat. They were graceful in zero-g, but atmosphere made maneuvers sluggish and acceleration slow. The gunships were faster and far more agile, but the *Raptor* had more cannons. Unfortunately, the gunships also had newer technology with automated targeting systems, while the torrents had to take more time to manually aim and shoot.

The *Raptor* was taking a beating, but she was giving as good as she got. Nonstop cannon fire blasted out from its eight gunners, keeping the gunships scurrying to evade. As one gunship was destroyed, more incoming appeared on screen.

Reyne focused on firing at every bogey that came within his range, while throwing quick glimpses to see that no gunships remained in the vicinity of the Citadel. The *Raptor* had done her job. "Praise the eversea," he said softly, and fired again.

When he noticed a limping gunship turn onto a suicidal course with the *Raptor*, he lined up his cannon and fired. The ship exploded, blinding him momentarily. His eyesight returned for him to see his system flashing a "Malfunction" warning. He'd lost all control of his cannon. With a grimace, he unbuckled and sprang from his seat to find another gun.

The *Raptor* tilted, throwing Reyne against a wall. He grunted and shoved off, trying to run at the steep angle. The nearest gunner's chair was a photon gun not far from the hull breach. He strapped in to find the system screen broken, but the gun felt operational in his grip.

He swung the gun around and laid down strafing fire at a pair of gunships that were making a wide bank for the stern. Several shots connected and bumped the ships off their course, but their shields held. The sliver of time it took for them to line back up their course cost them when a cannon blast shot out from the back of the ship and blew up one of the gunships. The exploding ship slammed into its wingman, sending the other ship careening out of control and crashing into the ground below in an explosion of its own.

Another blast rocked the warship.

"We've lost directional gyros, and our engines are overheating," Seda announced. *"Prepare for a hard landing."*

Reyne scanned the sky but saw nothing. He looked down at his broken screen and frowned. "How many bogeys do we have left?" he shouted to no one in particular.

"Three," came Critch's reply. "Lining up for a strafing run at our bow."

Reyne held on as the ship nosed down and descended. The sounds of photon blasts erupted through the ship, starting at the front and working their way back. The *Raptor* lurched and rolled to the side, giving Reyne a view of the night sky. Cannon fire responded.

Without any visual cue, he had no time to prepare for impact. All forward momentum stopped in an instant. His head slammed into the seat. Searing pain blossomed in his left hand.

When he regained his bearings, Reyne noticed the back of his hand was already swelling and bruising from smacking against the metal hull at the time of impact. He gingerly made a fist to make sure nothing was broken.

Out of the corner of his eye he caught movement. Pain was

forgotten as he grabbed the joystick, lined up the gun, and held down the trigger. The shots hit the gunship's nose. Its shields must've been compromised, because he watched his shots go right through the ship's view panel and take out the pilot. The dead ship flew straight at Reyne. His eyes widened, knowing there was no way to unbuckle in time.

By some miracle the dead pilot must've fallen forward, because the ship suddenly took an abrupt nose dive, crashing into the ground just before it would've struck the warship.

Reyne's jaw loosened as he leaned forward to peer out at the close call.

"The last two are bugging out," Critch yelled. "It looks like they've had enough for now."

They'll be back soon, with reinforcements. Reyne grimaced as he unbuckled and pushed himself from his seat. The ship was lying at an angle so that he could see some of the horizon and much of the night sky. He walked carefully down the angled hallway toward the front of the ship, using the railing for support. He met Boden in the hallway. "Are you injured?"

"I'm good," Boden replied.

The pair migrated to Sixx's gunner's chair to find it empty. "Sixx?" Reyne called out.

"With Maddox," he replied. "We could use a bit of help here."

Reyne and Boden hustled to find Sixx examining a metal beam that had fallen across Maddox's seat. Reyne put a hand on Maddox's shoulder to find him conscious.

"His leg's being pinched by the beam. It's probably broken, but I'm not seeing any blood," Sixx offered. "Once we cut through it, we should be good."

Maddox's eyes grew wide. "You're not cutting off my leg."

Sixx grinned. "I was talking about cutting through the beam, but now that you mention it, cutting through your leg would be a whole lot easier."

Reyne turned to Boden. "The mechanicals room is directly below the engine room in the aft of the ship. Think you can find a saw?"

Boden nodded. "I'll be right back."

"Move fast, because I don't know how long we have before more of our CUF friends show up."

Boden nodded again and took off at an awkward run down the uneven hallway.

Reyne looked from Maddox to Sixx. "You got this? I need to check on the others."

Maddox held up his thumb, and Sixx answered. "We're good."

Reyne headed down the hallway, but only took a few steps before he saw Critch and his team heading his way. Alex was nursing his arm, and Birk had his shirt tight around his head, a line of blood down his cheek. Critch and Nat looked otherwise unharmed.

"What's your team's status?" Critch asked.

"Maddox is pinned with a leg injury, but not in critical condition. Boden and Sixx are working at freeing him now. Otherwise, we're good. You?"

"We're good," Critch answered and then tapped Nat. "Go, help out with Maddox."

Reyne pointed. "They're right down there."

Nat hustled down the hallway.

Reyne glanced to the steps. "I haven't heard from the bridge yet."

Critch's lips thinned, and he followed Reyne down the stairs.

Reyne paused in his steps when he reached the bridge. It looked like the entire battle had taken place there. Black char indicated how many direct photon hits the bridge had taken. The view panel was fractured, with several holes through it. The stench of burning electrical and smoke filled Reyne's nostrils. In the center of the bridge, Hari was kneeling in front of Seda, who still sat in the captain's chair. A first aid kit lay at her feet, with the contents strewn about. Several empty syringes lay nearby.

Reyne hustled inside, and he heard the others rush in behind him. Hari looked up. Her hair was burnt and her shoulder was clearly dislocated, but she continued using her good arm as she tied white gauze around Seda's right arm...or what was left of it. His arm dangled by a few sinews. Blood pooled on the floor, but it looked like some of his arm had been charred enough to staunch the bleeding so that he was still conscious. A black streak showed the path a photon blast had burned across the floor and right up to the captain's chair, cutting through the arm of the chair and abruptly stopping.

"Lucky bastard," Critch said.

"He's nearly ready to be moved," she said, motioning them in. "Our pickup should be arriving any minute. We need to move quickly."

Seda glanced up with drug-filled eyes. He was pale and sweaty. "Hell of a fight, huh?"

Reyne forced a smile as he and Critch lifted the man from his seat.

Seda grimaced. "Leading from the shadows is far easier on one's health."

"It is." Reyne looked outside in the direction of the Citadel. "But I'm glad you stepped out of the shadows to do what needed to be done."

CHAPTER 15

HARD LESSONS

REYNE AND CRITCH took over Seda's hangar lounge so that they could apprise Heid of the recent events and their current predicament. She wasn't too happy, to put it mildly.

Heid's exasperated sigh came through the screen loud and clear. *"We've got the* Arcadia. *We can be there in four days. It's foolish to let a warship sit rusting out here when you need help on Terra."*

Critch growled. "The *Arcadia* is no match against the armada Ausyar is sending to Terra as we speak. They'll get here long before you will. The moment you'd drop out of jump speed, they'd fire everything they have at you. You'd get yourself killed, and we'd lose our best weapon against the CUF."

She pursed her lips. *"Is that me or the* Arcadia *you're talking about?"*

"Take your pick," Critch replied.

"Then, let me call my friends in the CUF. Over a third of the fleet is loyal to Alluvia, not to Ausyar. If I make the call, they may be able to turn the tide."

"When it comes to allies, we can't count on 'maybes'," Critch countered.

"Critch is right," Reyne said. "If any other CUF officers support us, they'll likely demand us to openly pledge allegiance to Alluvia. The fringe may be aligned with Alluvia in wanting to stop Myr's power play, but everyone knows that Alluvia will step right into any power vacuum left by taking down Myr and the fringe will be no better off than we are now."

"In the colonists' eyes, there's no difference between Myr and Alluvia," Critch added. "They would just see us trading two overlords for one. At least with two, we all believe they temper each other's power bids somewhat."

Reyne nodded. "Whatever we do, our goal must always be to free the colonies from Collective oversight."

"Alluvia will never support that," Heid said.

"Then, they're our enemy, too," Critch said.

Heid frowned. *"We'll fail without their help."*

Reyne shook his head. "If we can't trust Alluvia, we can't ally with them. Not yet, anyway. The Uprising was always about the fringe, so we start there. It's time to announce our intentions. If we don't, then the CUF will simply spin whatever story they want, and I guarantee it won't make us look good. Heid, do you still have your news contact on Alluvia?"

"Yes."

"Can she get a story out on the Collective News? One that can't be edited or retracted?"

"She can, but she'll likely lose her job over it. The story better be good because it'll likely be the only one she'll be able to broadcast."

Reyne nodded. "Understood. I'll send you the script later today. Keep us posted so we can be ready for the aftermath. Tell your friend if she can pull this off, we'll do our best to protect her."

Heid cast him a sideways glance. *"You know as well as I do that none of us can protect her on Alluvia."*

"Well, then she'll need to get herself to the colonies where we can help her," Critch added.

Heid gave a tight nod. *"I'll make sure she understands, though I must say that we're running out of room at Tulan Base, what with all the recent refugees from Nova Colony."*

"That should be a temporary situation," Reyne said. "Now that Terra has shown her claws, Ausyar will be done playing with the Coast. He'll bring his armada to Terra."

"Did Aeronaut have any updates on how much blight Ausyar still has and if he's planning on using it?"

"No news on that front," Reyne said. "Though, I believe Aeronaut made a new enemy with Mason with the stunt he pulled last night."

"That's not good. We need him in the Founders."

"What's the status on the specters?" Critch asked, growing impatient.

"They're all accounted for. The Delilah is docked here right now for repairs, and the Ocelot is here to pick me up. The others scattered after bringing in the refugees, per our original plan. But every single one of them is ready to head to Terra the moment you make the call."

"I know," Critch said. "Tell them to hold tight."

"I need to get back. The Ocelot is running and ready for launch. I'll be offline for the next ten days to resolve the matter we discussed earlier. Tell Aeronaut I'm glad to see he's finally stepping up to help, but he should've done that a long time ago. Then we wouldn't be in the mess we're in now."

When the screen went blank, Critch spoke. "I don't think she's Seda's biggest fan."

Reyne nodded. "Definitely not, but she took the news better than I expected. Far better than Throttle took the news when I told her I was better off staying on the surface for now rather than trying to make a run for it. I think the only thing that kept her from coming down here was sending her and Boden out to cover Heid's back."

Critch chuckled. "Funny, Gabe was more than happy to stay on the *Honorless* and leave me down here." He sighed. "Boden, Grundy, and Burl should be back on board our ships by now."

"Let's hope the CUF doesn't decide to start running patrols around the moons."

"They won't waste resources going after the one-offs. They'll focus everything they've got on us poor saps down here on Terra."

Reyne rolled his head to release tension. "We've been relying on luck for too long. It was bound to run out on us sometime."

"Speaking of luck, here comes someone who seems to never run out."

He turned to see Seda enter the hangar lounge. He was walking slowly and gingerly, but he was in one piece—upgraded with a rilon arm.

"He gets a new arm, and I can't even get a damn wrist comm," Critch grumbled.

"I'll have a tech bring a comm for you later today," Seda replied.

"It'd better be a Lotus G600 model with all the possible upgrades," Critch responded.

"I assumed as much."

Reyne nodded to the stationmaster's arm. "How's it feel?"

Seda moved it and winced. "It still feels like I'm lugging a lead weight around, but I suppose I'll get used to it. The doctors prefer to wait three days before attaching prosthetics; however, I thought it was in my best interest to have it attached immediately, considering the CUF will likely remove me from office and seize all my assets before then."

"You think they'll pin the Citadel on you?" Reyne asked.

Seda took a seat. "I'm sure they'll try, but they won't find any proof."

"You sure that shiny new arm of yours isn't proof enough?" Critch countered.

"This?" Seda lifted his arm a couple inches. "Didn't you hear? I lost my arm when the EMP hit Rebus Station and my cruiser crashed. The story's already in the news. It was a tragedy, really. That was my favorite cruiser."

Reyne's brow rose. "You're pretty quick at weaving stories."

"It's my job." Seda waved him off. "Besides, I'm not worried about the CUF. They can claim my assets—at least the ones they know about here on Terra—and I'll just disappear with a new identity. The bigger risk is Mason. His reach is farther and deeper than the CUF's. He'll do his best to see that I'm removed as a threat. He'll first create a reason for me to be on the CUF's watch list to make it harder for me to move around. Then he'll strike. I'm on a short timetable to build a defense strategy. This Citadel situation may have prevented me from leaving Terra today, what with all the interviews I have to give. I need to get off world to pick up my associates before Mason gets to them."

"While you're doing that, we need to get a Terran base of operations up and running," Reyne said. "We can't just sit around and wait for the CUF to find us."

"Use the hangar. The only way they'd discover this location is through pure luck," Seda said.

"It's not your hangar I'm worried about the CUF finding," Reyne argued.

Seda cocked his head. "Ah, you're talking about Broken Mountain. The tunnel entrances have all been hidden. My quarry companies set up gravel piles and other camouflage in front of each entrance. As for the mountain itself, the entire Collective believes its tunnels were destroyed twenty years ago.

The people are safe in the tunnels as long as they want to stay there."

"The challenge is, we can't make them stay there," Reyne said. "For any who want to leave, what do we do? If we force them to stay there, we've created another prison."

"We can't use the mountain as our base of operations. If we do, we may as well bring our own caskets," Critch said. "Having a single base is what caused us to lose the first Uprising. We need to be on the move constantly, working from multiple bases. Like Tulan Base on Playa. Like this hangar. The mountain can be used as a refugee camp, but it can't be one of our operating bases. Everyone stays there at their own risk."

"I support that strategy," Seda began, "but it'll take time to set up the infrastructure throughout the Collective. More importantly, we need to plan for every possible scenario. If we don't have escape routes, it'll be too easy for us to be cornered on a single planet, like what's happening right now. As for this hangar, it doesn't have any kind of defensive systems. Other than the holographic cover I needed for the *Raptor*, this is just a private airstrip. Nothing special.

"Oh, I wouldn't call this *just* a private airstrip," Critch said as he looked out into the hangar, where all the cannons and guns were laid out after being stripped off the *Raptor*.

"Having multiple bases is necessary," Reyne said. "It will take planning and someone with connections across the Collective." He turned to Seda.

Seda held up his hand. "Planning like that takes years. It takes networks, trades, and compromises."

"You have a strategic mind." Reyne's said, carefully watching the stationmaster. "Which is exactly why we need you in the Uprising."

"It's no different than what you've already been doing. Just now, you'll be doing it in an official capacity. No more shadow games," Critch said.

Seda frowned. "Any successful strategy always has shadow games. However, yes, I will help."

Critch walked over to a cabinet in the lounge and pulled out a bottle of Terran whiskey.

"How'd you know I had that there?" Seda asked.

Critch gave a small smile. "To the Uprising." He took a drink and handed the bottle to Seda. "Though I prefer a good bourbon any day over whiskey."

Seda ignored him and held up the bottle. "First strategy is to come up with a better name. There are too many negative emotions associated with the past." He drank and passed the bottle.

Reyne took the bottle. "How about the Fringe Liberation Campaign?"

Critch grimaced. "That's not a good name at all."

Seda shrugged and grabbed the bottle back. "Who knows? It could stick. To the Fringe Liberation Campaign."

CHAPTER 16

FLOODWATERS

IT WAS WELL past time they returned to Broken Mountain, though everyone dreaded it.

Reyne, Critch, and Seda left the hangar in a holo-cloaked sport vehicle. Sixx, Birk, and Hari rode along to provide protection from the Citadel refugees. Reyne found that the idea that they may need protection from those who'd once served as torrents in their army left a sour taste in his mouth.

But he had to remind himself that a lot had changed since the Uprising.

The vehicle pulled up to where a tunnel entrance had stood twenty years ago. Now, all he saw was the rocky side of a mountain. The driver held out a remote, the rock lifted, and Reyne realized it was a manufactured wall designed to blend into the surrounding terrain.

"I can see why your quarries haven't been profitable," Critch said. "You've invested in some high-end gadgets."

"Gadgets and ships have always been a passion of mine," Seda replied. "Any time I can dabble in them without the Collective's peering gaze, I find it more pleasurable."

The tunnel before them was a dark maw, threatening to swallow anyone who dared enter. His heart beat faster as memories resurfaced of nights of driving—sometimes running with a fallen comrade draped over his shoulder—into this tunnel following a battle or reconnaissance. The Uprising had left him with claustrophobia; he disliked entering the tunnels as much now as he did back then.

He supposed some things hadn't changed since the Uprising.

As they entered the large tunnel, Hari scrolled through her wrist comm, filling them in on the current situation. "About a third of the freed prisoners fled on foot rather than taking the transports to the tunnels. We've made no attempt to track them down or help them. We expect most who fled will likely be caught by the CUF patrols and killed, but our hands are already full with the ones who've accepted our help. For the refugees under our protection, we logged 12,698 in the tunnels, but twelve died overnight—one suicide, two cardiac arrests, and nine from injuries sustained during or after their escape. We've set up medical units, psychiatric units, control units, and isolation units for those needing help.

"The rest are in the general population, split among the tunnels. All the bathrooms and cafeterias are running at one hundred percent, but we're maxed out in the bunks since that project hadn't yet been completed. As anticipated, we've had unrest and acts of violence, but in general, things are going as well as can be expected. However, we anticipate a tepid response to your arrival. Most of these people are worn out from years of mental and physical abuse, and being back in the mountain seems to have made them very edgy."

Critch eyed Reyne. "I better take the lead."

Reyne grimaced and gave a nod before lifting the cloth up from his neck to cover his mouth and nose. Rather than wearing the itchy cloned skin, he had chosen to wear a shemagh to tour the mountain. Cloned skin would simply be a stopgap to bide time, but if he was going to be a leader he had to reveal his true face to his torrents sometime.

Everyone unloaded from the vehicle, and Reyne eyed the rifle Sixx carried. "Try not to look aggressive. We want to keep everyone as calm as possible."

"Good luck with that," Sixx said.

"Some may try to kill you," Critch added.

Reyne nodded. "I know."

Seda added, "I still recommend that you let them acclimate to freedom a bit longer before you meet with them."

"We have forces maintaining control in the tunnels who will be watching out for you," Hari said. "However, should you encounter any life-threatening situations, run back to the vehicle. Tax will stay with it while you're inside."

"We'll be fine. Anyone going after Reyne has to go through me first," Critch said, and walked forward.

They headed down the tunnel, walking straight toward the largest room in the mountain's system. It was a room they knew well. They'd briefed many missions here. The noise and smells of a large number of humans increased as they drew closer. Sixx tightened his position next to Reyne.

The moment they entered the cavernous room filled with people sitting on blankets, standing in place, or walking around, silence fell and everyone turned.

"It's Marshal Drake Fender!" someone shouted.

Critch raised his hand in recognition without a hitch in his step as they continued toward the center of the cavern.

"Marshal Fender!" another yelled. "We knew you'd come for us!"

Reyne noticed the hint of pride that flashed across Critch's face at the mention of his real name, and suddenly he was pulled back two decades to when he and Critch led the torrents side by side—many of the same people—right here in Broken Mountain.

Very few paid any attention to Seda, which meant there must not have been news screens in the Citadel or else they'd all recognize his face. Those who did recognize Seda bowed their heads in respect, a sharp contrast from how many of his other counterparts were seen.

The six of them stopped in the center of the room.

Hari scanned the room with her comm. "There are roughly 3,500 people in here. The others are spread throughout the tunnels and in the units."

"It's a start. We'll hit the larger tunnels, and news will spread," Critch said, and waved a hand through the air to silence the room. He spoke loudly, his hard voice echoing off the walls. "You're free. The Citadel is done."

Everyone cheered.

He waved once more, and the room hushed. "You are free to stay here in the mountain for as long as you like. The CUF has no idea that these tunnels have been rebuilt by our friend here, Seda Faulk, stationmaster of Rebus Station."

Several cheers erupted for Seda, and Seda nodded with a polite smile.

"You are also free to go. No one's going to make the choice for you. I know staying in these tunnels is hard for those of you who've been here before. I know it's hard for me to be in them again. If you choose to leave, Stationmaster Faulk has guidance."

Critch turned to Seda, who stepped forward to speak. "We have been working to bring down the Citadel for some time, and we didn't have everything in place yet. I ask for your patience as we get a better support network set up for you. Within two days, we'll have a relocation unit established that will help you reconnect with your families and homes without drawing CUF attention. However, I highly recommend you stay in the tunnels for the time being for your safety. The CUF has implemented martial law and is hitting Rebus Station hard searching for escapees, and we'll keep you apprised of any major changes. I'll see that news screens are brought in so you can follow the news as well. I warn you that the Collective fully controls the news, so remember that when you see how the stories are spun. If you choose to leave on your own, contact someone wearing a blue armband and they can arrange transportation for you to a location where there are no CUF patrols. In the meantime, welcome to Broken Mountain."

Hari busily jotted down notes as he spoke.

Critch then continued. "Broken Mountain is not a military base. It is a place for you to recover and stay while the CUF is out there causing problems. I know many of you were torrents before. You've more than served your time, so we shouldn't ask more of you, but we will. We're rebuilding the torrent army, and we can use each and every one of you. Unlike the Collective, we don't conscript. We only take volunteers. If you'd like to enlist—or reenlist—talk to anyone wearing an armband for more details. Most of you know me, and you'll get to know Stationmaster Faulk, who's providing extensive support." He paused and looked at Reyne. "And, I imagine you remember Marshal Aramis Reyne, who's leading this campaign with me."

Gasps and denials had filled the room by the time Reyne lowered his shemagh to reveal his face. Angry yells quickly followed.

"Traitor!"

Reyne ducked some object thrown directly at his head. Sixx jumped in front of him as a human shield.

Critch moved next to Reyne and put a hand on his shoulder. "Hear me out! Marshal Reyne is no traitor. He was sitting in a CUF prison when the attack on Broken Mountain occurred."

"That's when he betrayed us," someone shouted.

Critch waved to silence the crowd, but many kept talking "The real traitor of Terra was found and killed. If Marshal Reyne was the traitor, you don't think I would've killed him myself?"

The last statement was yelled, and the discord began to dissipate. Only when the room quieted did Critch continue. "I trust Marshal Reyne with my life. He did not betray us, nor would he ever betray our cause. I would not stand alongside him if I suspected otherwise. He was the greatest leader the Uprising ever had, and many of you followed him through hell and back. *I* followed him. If you believe the rumors and you don't trust him, then you don't trust me, and you shouldn't reenlist. However, if you can move past rumors and gossip and believe in what we're trying to accomplish here, then we welcome you."

Critch motioned to Reyne, who took a breath before speaking. "There's not a day that goes by that I don't think about the lives lost during the Uprising, or the years you've spent in a CUF prison because you stood up for those who couldn't stand up for themselves. We were betrayed, and it hurt. It still hurts. I find myself thinking, 'What if we weren't betrayed and we'd won the Uprising?'"

He shook his head before continuing. "But that line of thinking is weak, because there's nothing that can be done to change the past. What we can change is the future. We can change things so that our children aren't conscripted into CUF service when they turn eighteen. We can change things so that we can own property or visit family in another colony without having to buy a Collective pass-card. We can change the future because we're torrents."

He paused briefly as he found the comfortable pace that he'd often used with the torrents long ago. "I don't know if all of you have heard the story behind why we came up with the name 'torrents.' It came from a small colony here on Terra. The colony was called New Liberty. Any of you heard of it?"

Several raised their hands.

"New Liberty had broken Collective law. They set up a school in a shed behind a farmer's house. As you're aware, only Collective-funded schools are legal, but the Collective won't provide resources to most colonies. When a conscripted colonist from New Liberty was discovered reading a book, the CUF sent in a squad to burn down the school and make arrests. Unknown to the squad, it had rained a hundred miles north of New Liberty a couple days earlier. By rain, I mean it was a *torrential* downpour.

"As you know already, Terra is mostly one big desert, so when it rains it tends to cause these massive flash floods that swoop through, and then everything dries up again. Well, to get to the New Liberty, the squad had to first cross a deep valley. Wouldn't you know, when they got halfway across that valley, the floodwaters came crashing through. When the waters cleared a few minutes later, there was no sign of that squad. It was as if the torrents came through to set things right. And that's why we took on the name 'torrents' to represent our army. We torrents will crash through the Collective and set things right. I'm a torrent. Who else here is a torrent?"

Critch stepped forward. "I'm a torrent."

Seda also stepped forward, throwing Reyne a glance. "I'm a torrent."

Someone from the crowd yelled, "I'm a torrent!" Sixx, Birk, and Hari all chimed in. The phrase was soon echoed by others until the room was chanting "torrents" over and over.

With the room still chanting, the six departed into a tunnel.

"I don't think you'll need the shemagh anymore," Critch said quietly as they began their journey through the smaller tunnels.

"Aramis Reyne," someone called out from behind them.

Reyne tensed, expecting an assault. When none came, he turned slowly to face a man hobbling toward them.

"Do you recognize me?" the man asked.

Reyne narrowed his gaze as he tried to place the man through the full gray scraggly beard. It was the blue eyes that made him remember, and Reyne realized the man wasn't nearly as old as he looked.

"I do." Reyne cocked his head. "I'd always wondered what happened to you. You were in the news constantly, and then you just disappeared."

"It seems my beliefs weren't in line with my superiors'."

"I didn't realize they sent citizens to the Citadel."

"There are more of us sent there than you realize. Anyone who gets in the way of the wrong person faces the threat of the Citadel. It's good motivation to always follow the rules. Citizens and colonists have feared the Citadel for too long. Its collapse was welcomed across the Collective."

Reyne paused. "I suppose I should introduce you. Everyone, meet Commandant Jed Baptiste of the Collective Unified Forces."

"You shouldn't say it so loud," the old man said. "You of all people know that names carry weight."

"The destroyer of Broken Mountain," Critch said. "Now I recognize you. You led the final battle that crushed the Uprising."

Baptiste spoke with a sad intonation in his voice. "I believed I was serving the greater cause. I've learned much since then."

"It was Commandant Baptiste's brig that I was in during the final days of the Uprising. Doc provided the intel on Broken Mountain to him," Reyne said.

"You set up Reyne to be seen as a traitor," Critch said.

"You know how much crap this man has had to deal with because of you?" Sixx added. "That was a pretty low thing to do."

Baptiste held up his hands in surrender. "That was never my intention. The thought had never even crossed my mind at the time. I didn't release Marshal Reyne to be a scapegoat. I released him and cleared his record so that a little girl would have a father."

Reyne clasped the man's frail shoulders, his heart wrenching at how the strong CUF officer he couldn't help but respect during the Uprising had become a shadow of his former self. "I know why you did it. I never held it against you."

"Thank you," Baptiste replied quietly.

Reyne watched the citizen for a moment. "You're a free man now. What will you do?"

He shook his head. "I have nowhere to go. I could never return to Alluvia. My family believes I'm dead."

Reyne shot a quick glance at Critch before speaking. "You could become a torrent," he offered. "You have a wealth of military knowledge and training," Reyne said. "We can always use another advisor."

Baptiste looked at Critch. "I doubt that offer extends to citizens, especially those who've served in the CUF."

"The offer stands," Critch snapped. "Everyone's equal in the fringe. But you'll find no special treatment for being a citizen, and you'll be held to the same standard as any torrent."

After a moment, Baptiste stood taller, suddenly looking several years younger. "I'd be honored to serve the torrent army in any capacity you see fit."

Seda motioned to a man wearing a blue armband, who happened to be walking by. "We have a torrent recruit. Officer level. Help get him signed up."

The man nodded and stepped up to Baptiste. "I'll get you processed."

"Thank you," Baptiste said to Reyne. His blue eyes shimmered with tears.

A sense of rightness filled Reyne's heart, and he found himself smile. "I'm glad we came here today."

"Our army is going to be quite the collection of strays and mutts," Critch said.

"That it is," Reyne said with confidence. "And that's one of the reasons why we'll win."

As he and his compatriots continued down the tunnels, he felt Sixx watching him. "What is it?" Reyne asked.

"That guy released you so you could take care of Throttle," Sixx said.

Reyne nodded. "If he hadn't done what he did, neither Throttle nor I would be alive today."

"I guess knowing that takes the sting off a bit at being seen as a traitor," Hari said.

"No. Not at all," Reyne replied.

At that moment they passed by an adjoining tunnel, and Critch stopped cold. Then he smiled, turned, and strolled down that tunnel.

"Where's he going?" Seda asked. "The medical unit is this way."

When Reyne recognized the old torrent, he pulled out his pistol. "Retribution."

Sixx noticed Reyne's actions and unslung his rifle. Birk already had his pistol in his hand. Hari and Seda gave each other a look before pulling out their weapons.

"Mingh," Critch said as he approached the man.

The man turned and immediately grinned. "Marshal Fender, it's an honor to see you."

"I've been looking for you."

Mingh held his fingers to his chest in surprise. "Me? I heard the torrent hoorah speech in there. You sound as good as ever, but if you're looking to bring me into your new army, I've got to think on it."

Critch pulled a knife and sliced Mingh's throat before the man had a chance to react. Mingh fell to his knees, clutching his throat. Mingh's men pulled their shivs, but immediately backed off when they saw the guns leveled on them.

Critch stood over Mingh, wiping his blade clean. "I would never have you in my army. That man you killed a couple days ago in the Citadel? He was a very good friend and an even better torrent. You?" Mingh toppled to the floor. "You're nothing except dead."

When Critch returned, Reyne eyed him. "Feel better?"

"No. He got off too easy."

Reyne clapped his shoulder. "Maybe seeing Vym will cheer you up."

Critch shot him a look. "She's likely pissed at us for taking so long to break her out of that hellhole."

Reyne frowned. "You're right. She's not going to be in a good mood."

CHAPTER 17

BATTLE LINES

"TOOK you long enough to stop by for a visit," Vym said from her bed in a private room off the infirmary.

The woman had aged far too much in the last year, Reyne noticed as he and Critch approached. Each man grabbed one of her hands.

After a moment, her scowl relaxed. "It's good to see you two together again. I've been out of the loop for a year. You'll have much to fill me in on...but I'm tired. It'll have to be later."

"I hope you haven't grown too attached to this place," Seda said as he took a seat on her cot next to her. "I'm having you moved to a new location today."

"Seda, my dear man." Vym smiled at Seda as he bent over and kissed her cheek. "I never doubted you'd come for me."

He seemed insulted. "I'd never leave one of my own to rot in that place."

She guffawed. "If all it took was for me to get thrown into prison for you to get off your lazy butt and take down that awful place, then my time there was well served." She patted his hand.

"Thank you for sending in that pair of nice looking men to come fetch me. I admit I don't think I could've made it to the buses."

"I'm only sorry I couldn't have been there to take you to my personal clinic. I never meant for you to be brought here. But some matters arose that I needed to take care of first."

She frowned as she examined his rilon arm. "Does that have anything to do with the rumors I keep hearing of a ghost ship fighting off a squadron of CUF gunships?"

Seda chortled. "Everyone knows ghost ships aren't real."

She shot him a sideways glance. She then looked up at the others standing around her. "Hari, my girl. Good to know Seda hasn't driven you off yet."

"No, ma'am," the woman replied with a smile.

Birk gave a small wave. "Hi, Stationmaster Patel."

"Hello, Birk. I see Critch still isn't giving you enough to eat."

Sixx approached, and she scowled. "Oh no you don't. You stay back there. I'm still upset with you."

He held up her hands. "I didn't know she was your niece at the time. I swear it."

"Tut, tut, I don't want to hear it. You are an incorrigible young man. You'd better watch yourself. I'll be back on my feet in no time, and then you'll be sorry."

Seda's tablet chimed, and all heads turned to him. He pulled it out of his pocket and declined the call. "He can leave a message," he muttered.

Vym looked at the gray tablet and then across the faces. "My, times have changed even more than I realized."

"I'll bring you up to speed after I return from Myr," Seda said.

"Myr?" Sixx asked, before quickly tacking on, "I'm going with you."

"I won't be there long enough for you to see anything. I'm

landing to pick someone up, and then I'll be heading back to the fringe."

"That's fine," Sixx said. "I'm still going with you."

Seda shrugged. "So be it." His tablet beeped, and he looked at it. He stared at the screen, frowning.

"Seda, what is it? What's wrong?" Vym asked.

He slowly looked up and blinked as though his mind had been in a different place. "Mason sent me a picture of him sitting in my office in Rebus Station."

"He's here?" Critch asked.

"You can't go, Seda," Reyne said. "You know it's a trap."

"I know that," Seda gritted out. He turned to Hari.

"I'll check it out," she said quickly.

"I'll go with you," Critch offered. "Mason and I have some unfinished business to discuss."

"No," Seda ordered. "If Mason's here, he'll be surrounded by dromadiers. You'll be shot on sight."

Critch narrowed his eyes. "I can get around a few droms."

Seda shook his head. "You don't stand a chance going after Mason on his terms. He's too good."

"He's right," Vym added. "You would die today if you walked into one of his traps."

"I survived last time," Critch retorted. He took a deep breath and pursed his lips. "Fine. But I will get him. It's only a matter of time."

"*We* will take him down," Reyne corrected.

"Go, Hari. Be careful," Seda said. "Who knows what Mason has planned."

Hari nodded. "I'll see you back at the hangar."

Seda watched Hari rush away before he turned to Vym. "Let's get you out of here."

The woman pushed herself into a sitting position, setting off a coughing fit. After drinking some water, she spoke. "Best thing I've heard all day."

The journey from the mountain was quiet and tense. When they reached the hangar, Seda paced the floor nonstop until Hari returned. She pointed at the lounge for him to join her there. He strode over but, before closing the door, motioned for Critch and Reyne to follow.

"He wasn't there," she began. "The CUF has taken over Rebus Station and turned it into a military base per Corps General Ausyar's orders. I had to use your back entrance to bypass all the security. Some commandant was already taking over your office when I arrived."

"Now that Rebus Station is under martial law, I anticipated Ausyar would ensure I have as little reason as possible to get in their way."

"The officer gave this to me to give to you. He said Mason left it for you."

He took the silver box from her hands and ran his fingers over the ornate pattern. "Did you open it?"

She paused. "Yes. I wanted to make sure it wasn't a bomb or poison."

He swallowed and lifted the lid. His jaw clenched tight and his lower lip trembled as he gently reached in and pulled out the contents.

Reyne couldn't make out what he was holding, but whatever it was seemed to traumatize the powerful man. Reyne stepped over. "What is it?"

Seda plopped onto the couch, still holding the contents. He gazed up briefly before looking back down at the item that lay across his palm.

At first Reyne thought the item was a piece of leather with markings on it. His lips parted when he realized it was human. The bluish hue of the skin narrowed it down to someone from Myr. "Who's it from?"

Seda swallowed. "Every Founder has three brands." He touched each marking as he spoke.

"Each rune represents an equal branch of the Founders—towers for Alluvia, waves for Myr, and wings for the colonies." He ran his finger across the fourth marking. "Only three Founders have a fourth brand that reads 'tribus' in Latin, which means 'three'. It's for the Founders who oversee one of each of the three branches."

He exhaled. "I oversee the colonies. Mariner oversees Myr, and Mason oversees Alluvia. I know it's from Mariner because she had a birthmark just below her brands. Right here." He pointed to a spot on his lower abdomen. His almost-smile was erased by him fighting back tears.

He clutched the skin and the box and pushed to his feet. "Mason just launched his coup to take over the Founders. He'll be coming for me next." He strode from the lounge without another word.

After a lengthy pause where no one moved or spoke, Hari walked over, poured herself a glass of whiskey, and took a seat. "He loved her very much. They'd been together for as long as I knew him. I think they'd even married in secret, though he never admitted it."

"Mason knew how to hit Seda where it hurt most," Reyne said. "It's what Mason does."

"We'll make sure he pays for his crimes," Critch said.

She held up her glass. "I can drink to that."

Reyne watched Hari for a moment. "You're a Founder, too, aren't you?"

She looked up. "I suppose secrets are unnecessary in this

room. Yes, I'm a Founder. I'm Mechanic. I was assigned to Aeronaut to help him 'fix' things." She chuckled drily. "I always hated that name. I'm awful around anything mechanical."

Critch frowned. "How many of you are there?"

She shook her head sadly and looked down at her glass. "Our numbers seem to be declining by the hour."

They remained in the lounge for the next couple of hours talking and drinking—sharing old stories and planning for the future. By the time Seda returned, his usual stoic face was in place. Neither the silver box nor the skin was anywhere in sight.

He strode across the room to the large screen and punched in several codes. He glanced over his shoulder. "I'll get you the full resources of Terra for the campaign."

He turned back to his screen and went live. "This is Stationmaster Seda Faulk with a message to all Faulk associates and Rebus Station confederates. Martial law was illegally enacted by Corps General Ausyar of the CUF Armada, and I will not stand for that. Under my authority, Terra wartime protocols are enacted, effective now. All Rebus teams are called into duty. All Category Five resources are approved for transfer. All communications should be made through Rebus channel eighty-eight. The Rebus reclamation effort is now in effect. The CUF will attempt to suppress our rights, but we will show the Collective that Terrans are not slaves. It is time for Terra to establish its independence."

He clicked off the screen, grabbed the half-empty bottle of whiskey off the table, and took a seat, facing the slack-jawed trio. "The key to winning a war is fighting on multiple fronts. The first front is here on Terra, and the battle starts now. We'll set up fronts on every fringe world, and then we'll bring the war to Alluvia and Myr. Mason's going to have his hands full if he thinks he can suppress our rebellion."

Reyne stared, wide-eyed.

Critch cocked his head. "Well, I think you got Mason's attention."

"Along with every other person in the Collective," Reyne added, "since I have no doubt the hackers will make sure your declaration of war is broadcast across every channel."

Seda looked at them. "I hope you're ready to lead an army, because it's time."

Reyne frowned, then nodded. "I am, but I'm going to have to break some bad news to Sixx. He won't be happy that his side project must be delayed."

"I heard about his situation," Critch said. "That's rough."

"I can get him a lift to Myr if that's what he wants," Seda said. "But I'll need to pair him with a Myrad, or else he'll be arrested if he gets caught walking alone. Have him talk to Hari if he's interested in going through with it. Though it's a bad time for anyone to be traveling right now, especially a colonist."

Reyne gave a small tilt of his head. "I'll let him know."

Critch came to his feet and walked over to Seda and Hari, where he dropped something in each of their laps. "These belong to you."

Hari dangled her chain in the light. "It's the torrent teardrop."

"Every torrent has one," Critch said.

Reyne added, "And you two have more than earned the right to wear it."

"I'll wear it with pride," she said and slid it over her head.

Seda had been staring at his in his palm. He weakly smiled before slipping it over his head and tucking it in his shirt. "It's a good symbol."

Reyne's wrist comm vibrated. When he read the message, his jaw tightened. "Turn on the Collective channel."

"Play DZ-Five," Seda said, and the large screen came to life.

This is Lina Tao reporting for DZ-Five News.

You have just seen the startling war declaration made by Stationmaster Seda Faulk of Terra, announcing that Terra would be a free world. The declaration was made after the Collective Unified Forces, under command of Corps General Ausyar, initiated martial law in Rebus Station. A projected 274 colonists have been killed in the first day. This action was in response to a group of colonists breaking into the Citadel to free prisoners who were allegedly being kept there without a right to a fair trial.

The group—who call themselves fringe torrents—freed the political prisoners from the Citadel as the first step in what they're calling the Fringe Liberation Campaign. They demand Parliament to recognize each fringe planet as a free and independent citizen world.

The torrents continue to deny that they had any involvement in the creation of or the release of the blight last year, which they assert was released by the Founders, the clandestine organization believed to have gone defunct after the War. The torrents have shared the name of Gabriel Heid, chief magistrate of Alluvia, as the organization's leader and driver behind the creation and distribution of the blight. The torrents claim responsibility for acquiring and releasing the fungicide on Sol Base in their attempt to protect the colonies.

They also affirm that Ice Port was attacked wrongly and without provocation by the Collective Unified Forces under the purview of Corps General Michel Ausyar, with the intent to silence colonists speaking up against inequality.

This is Lina Tao reporting the truth. Let the colonies be free.

"I like her closing. It had a nice ring to it," Critch said and took a drink.

"She revised the script," Seda said. "But it works. I especially liked how she included Ausyar's and Heid's names. Their hands will be full dealing with questions."

Reyne shook his head, tension squeezing at his heart. "What she did was dangerous enough. Mentioning Ausyar and Heid was suicide. That poor woman's life expectancy just dropped to about sixty seconds."

"None of us like it, but death is an inevitable condition of rebellion," Seda said. "Sacrifices are made, and it's our job as leaders to make sure something good comes out of them."

"Thanks to Lina Tao," Critch began, "everyone across the Collective goes to bed tonight knowing that the galaxy has tilted on its axis and there's no going back."

"Between Lina's broadcast and mine, I'd say the Fringe Liberation Campaign is officially launched," Seda said. "We're going to have rebellions sparking in every colony within days, if not hours."

"The Fringe Liberation Campaign," Hari mused. "I like it. It's a good name for a war."

EPILOGUE

GABRIELA HEID ENTERED Devil Town's stationhouse like she didn't have a care in the world. Today, she wore the simple, scratchy CUF uniform assigned to all conscripts. She'd also lightened her hair and left it hang loose, though she still wasn't used to the sensation of hair on her shoulders.

One of the first lessons her father had taught was that the simplest disguises were often the most effective. She had to admit Mason was right about some things, such as espionage, assassinations, and torture. But he was terribly wrong about other things, especially the things that really mattered. Like freedom, equality, and the value of humanity.

Dozens of conscripts patrolled the stationhouse, and she blended in effortlessly. She scanned the fake pass-card and received a computer stick that led her through the crowd and to a door where she inserted the stick into the lock.

The computer stick emitted a masculine groan of ecstasy. *"You fit me into that slot wonderfully, Ms. Smyth. You may now proceed. May your visit to Devil Town fulfill all your fantasies."*

"It'll at least be a start," she murmured before she stepped out of the bustling room and into a winding corridor.

She continued until a tall, muscular man approached her. He looked her up and down appraisingly before giving her a smile that hinted at carnal promises.

Heid gave him a once-over and smiled in response because while he thought she was checking him out, she was scanning him for weapons. On the downside, he was carrying two pistols and a rather long knife. Nearly as many weapons that she had hidden under her uniform.

He motioned down the hallway. "If you'll come with me, I'll take you to see the stationmaster."

She could've sworn he'd said, "If you'll come *for* me." She tilted her head. "I'd like that very much."

Heid found the stationmaster sitting at his desk in an office that was outrageously gaudy. As soon as she entered, he stood and looked past her shoulder. "Leave us."

When the door closed behind her, she cast a glance to make sure they were alone. The stationmaster walked over to her and held out his hand. She masked her disdain of both the stationmaster and his décor by forcing a pleasant smile and giving him her hand.

"Gabriela, I've long since hoped to make your acquaintance," he said before bending over and kissing her hand. "Lincoln Finn, at your service."

He held onto her hand a second too long, but she let him linger.

"I've been looking forward to our visit," she said.

"Please have a seat, my dear." He returned to his desk and leaned back in his chair. "I have to admit. I'm surprised you came, especially after all that hoopla on the news lately."

She shrugged. "The CUF does make things a bit challenging,

but I hope that I have nothing to worry about while I'm in your care."

"You're perfectly safe here," he said all too quickly.

Her lips curled upward. "Captain Reyne assured me that I should meet with you."

"Did he, now?"

"He did."

Lincoln examined her smugly. "Well, I suppose you want to talk about how I can help your torrents out with—what is it that you're calling your little rebellion now? Oh, yes. The Fringe Liberation Campaign."

She shook her head. "No."

He leaned forward. "No? Why not?"

"We already know that you aren't going to support the Campaign. Not without keeping one hand in the Collective's coffers."

He frowned. "Then what are you doing here?"

Heid ran a finger sensually up her leg, and she noticed his gaze followed the motion. "I'd like to leave a message for Ausyar."

"I don't have any contact with Corps General Ausyar."

"You don't?" She cocked her head. "Funny, you told Reyne you did. And Seda seemed to think Ausyar paid you a hefty sum to lure me into a trap."

He stammered. "Nonsense. I have no idea what you're talking about. I simply preferred to negotiate with you instead of with an old traitor or a scarred pirate."

She unsheathed the knife hidden on her thigh and flung it at the stationmaster. The blade skewered Lincoln's eye and embedded deeply in his skull. The man was dead before he hit the floor.

She slid over his desk and searched the panel for the switch to lock the office door. Safely secure in the room, she glanced at her wrist comm and noted the three minutes she had before Ausyar's dromadiers would likely be crawling all over the place—assuming Lincoln had triggered an alarm when she'd first arrived.

Then, she plugged in a small computer stick into his computer panel and waited. When the light flashed green, which was the signal that the hacker had connected, she turned back to the body.

Heid tugged her knife free from his head, the movement making a wet sound as it pulled out of the eyeball. She cut open his shirt and carved her message to Ausyar... and more importantly, to her father.

Finished, she wiped the blade on Lincoln's shirt. She glanced at her comm. With nearly two minutes to spare, she stood and strolled right out the office's back door.

FRINGE CAMPAIGN

Book 3 in the Fringe Series

There is no turning back from war now.

The Fringe Liberation Campaign has sparked protests and rebellions across the Collective, forcing the three torrent captains--Reyne, Critch, and Heid--to be spread out across the fringe. Critch leads the Terran front, trying to stop the Collective Unified Forces from attacking the remaining fringe colonies. Reyne faces nearly impossible odds at uniting the fringe colonies into a single rebel force. And Heid runs missions to save refugees whose homes have been destroyed by the CUF.

Divided, they soon learn they don't stand a chance against the CUF. Terra falls. Reyne loses a crucial crewmember. Heid is seen as an enemy to both sides. Can they unite into a single front before the Collective sends everything they've got to end the Campaign and kill every last torrent?

Get *Fringe Campaign* today!

THE COLLECTIVE

The Collective is comprised of six terraformed planets in nearby solar systems within the Milky Way galaxy. The Collective is controlled by the dual leadership of Alluvia and Myr. Only those born on Alluvia and Myr are given legal status as citizens, while all others are considered colonists and receive fewer privileges. The Collective views colonists as means to achieve gain, and their pressure will drive the colonies—the fringe—to desperate actions.

MYR is a silver-rich, water-rich citizen world with idyllic islands. Myr was the first settled planet in the Collective. Myrads have argyria and take great pride in their blue-hued skin.

ALLUVIA is a water-covered citizen world and home to First City, the Collective's largest city. Alluvia was the second settled planet in the Collective, and has the highest gravity of all Collective worlds. Alluvia has thick cloud cover and frequent storms.

DARIOS is the most naturally habitable world and provides much of the Collective's food supply. As such, it's heavily regulated by the Collective. Its fringe station is Sol Base.

PLAYA is the furthest world from Alluvia and Myr. It has low gravity and freezing temperatures. Its fringe station is Ice Port, which was destroyed by the CUF.

SPATE is a desert-like world and has the largest fringe station, Devil Town, known for its massive garden.

TERRA is a battle-scarred world, where much of the Uprising took place. Its fringe station is Rebus Station. Terra, the planet nearest to Alluvia and Myr, is home to the Citadel, the Collective's high-security prison.

SPACE COAST is an asteroid belt outside Collective control and home to smugglers, pirates, and other outlaws. Its fringe station is Nova Colony, home to the infamous Uneven Bar.

GLOSSARY OF TERMS

ABYSS: *Term used to describe people and ships lost in space, presumed or known dead.*

CHIMESUIT: *Blue, armored space suit worn by dromadiers. Named for the chime-like sounds the suit emits.*

CITIZEN: *Free person born on Alluvia or Myr.*

COLONIST aka *Fringe: General population in the fringe. Considered impure and lesser by many citizens.*

COMM: *References communications sent/received, as well as personal communication devices.*

CUF: *Collective Unified Forces (CUF). The Collective's military led by Corps General Michel Ausyar.*

DRIFT: *Slang term, meaning to die or to kill. E.g., "I drifted him with a single shot to the head."*

DROMADIER: *Soldier in the Collective Unified Forces.*

EM FIELD: *Short for Electro Magnetic Field. On-ship technology to produce artificial gravity.*

EMP: *Short for Electro Magnetic Pulse. Weapon employed by the CUF to disable ships.*

EVERSEA: *A term referencing the space frontier. An Eden.*

FOUNDERS: *Secret organization of citizens and colonists who steer the Collective's actions using ulterior methods. Believed to have gone defunct after the War.*

FRINGE: *Refers to the tributary planets and colonists under Collective control (Darios, Playa, Spate, and Terra), as well as the Space Coast.*

FRINGE STATION: *A trading outpost with space docks. Located in the planet's largest colony.*

JUMP SPEED: *fastest speed at which ships currently travel. Requires jump shields to protect crews from hydrogen radiation poisoning from high, faster-than-light speeds.*

LOGGER: *Waterlogged "puffy" person addicted to seasoned water, i.e. water seasoned with sweet soy.*

PIRATE: *Outlaw who raids ships and smuggles contraband.*

RILON: *Extremely durable yet flexible metal used on most hulls, weapons, and tools.*

RUNNER: *Interstellar postman and transporter.*

Fringe runners commonly smuggle blue tea or sweet soy.

SOLAR SAILS: *Large flexible sails on ships used for long-haul space travel.*

STAR SWARM: *Tsunami of space garbage/debris pulled into an asteroid's gravitational pull.*

STRETCH: *Playan colonist with low-g mutations. Extremely tall, with respiratory and heart defects.*

SWEET SOY: *Highly addictive drug, often mixed with water.*

TENURED: *Indentured servant. Tenured are often tricked into servitude.*

TORRENT: *Colonist rebel who fought in the Uprising twenty years before the* Fringe Series *takes place.*

UPRISING: *A revolt by the fringe colonists against citizens of Alluvia and Myr for equal rights.*

VIG: *Derogatory term, referring to a small, smelly rodent found on Spate.*

VOICELESS: *Tenured who have had their vocal cords destroyed because they broke laws or attempted to escape servitude.*

The WAR: *War between Alluvia and Myr. The War ended with a truce and the creation of the Collective, as well as initiating the push for colonizing other worlds for resources.*

WOMBIE: *Mutated, slow-moving Spaten colonists who have developed a camel-like ability to store water. Have extremely low IQs.*

ABOUT THE AUTHOR

Rachel Aukes is the award-winning author of over thirty novels, including *100 Days in Deadland,* which made Suspense Magazine's Best of the Year list. She is also a Wattpad Star, her stories having over seven million reads. When not writing, she can be found flying old airplanes over the Midwest countryside and catering to an exceptionally spoiled fifty-pound lapdog.

Join Rachel's spam-free newsletter to be the first to hear about new releases: www.rachelaukes.com/join

ACKNOWLEDGMENTS

With extreme thanks to my editors, Stephanie Riva and Laurel Kriegler, for helping bring this story to life—and for your eleventh hour heroics. Also, a huge thanks goes out to my husband who patiently puts up with long writing hours and listening to all the crazy story ideas. Most of all, thank you, my readers, for your messages, cheers, and enthusiasm.

9 780989 901871